Dogs OF Summer

BY BRUCE CANOLES

"A call to arms against your fellow countrymen requires more than a just cause. To spill the blood of valiant men must only be the course of last resort."

General Harlan Buford Summer, C.S.A.

March 28, 1861

PROLOGUE

Summer County, Alabama   *Spring 1998*

She stared hard at the intricate spider webbing draped from the thick rafters of the old barn. The maze of webs captured afternoon rays of spring sunlight and dazzled like a multi-colored Christmas light display. Callie always intensely studied the profuse jungle of webs when she lay here. She had learned to let her mind escape to the freedom of the mystical space known only to spiders, barn owls and Callie.

It was almost over. It didn't hurt. It hadn't hurt much in over a year now. Just like always, he groaned loudly one last time as he slammed his body down on top of her small frame. The sweaty man pushed himself to his feet and pulled up his pants. Callie lay motionless and waited while he stepped into the leather boots and cinched his belt. When he nodded his head in her direction, she quickly scrambled back into her own clothes.

He smiled at her. "You sure look good with that new tan." Callie remained focused on buttoning her blouse and did not respond. He always tried to talk to her just after he finished. The sound of his voice made her cringe with revulsion. "Remember sweetie, don't you say nothing about this to your mama, Okay? You understand me, don't you?"

She nodded without speaking or looking at his grinning face. She felt better just realizing she would be with her mother in a short while.

ONE

The familiar ring of the school day's last bell set in motion a fateful episode that forever transformed the placid world of Summer County.

Near the venerable school's front entrance, a moss-covered stone monument proclaimed Summer High School was founded in 1918. In many ways, the school and the county had changed little in the ensuing eighty years. Some would say both were frozen in a quieter and more genteel time.

Inside the gray rock school building, the 3:00 bell vibrated loudly. Summer High principal Bester Dumas propped his feet on his cluttered desk and watched the stream of giddy students rush the buses. He fixed his gaze out his side window with his back to the closed office door. When Marabell Jordan burst into the room unannounced, Dumas jumped straight up knocking a stack of folders crashing to the floor.

"Bester, we have an emergency situation!" the plump history teacher shrilled, waving her short arms dramatically.

"Oh, my gosh, Marabell, what is it?" the principal asked as his bald forehead flushed red with worry.

"Bester, you better sit down for this!" Without waiting for him to find his chair, she continued speaking and flailing her arms. "You know I have several of those mountain children in my eighth grade homeroom. Well, everybody knows how *all* my pupils grow to love and trust me," she gushed as she folded her arms serenely across her large bosom. "This one precious child, Callie Baines, has just confided a *terrible* secret to me!" Marabell's expression turned somber and she unfolded her arms and shook a pointed finger in Dumas's direction. "We all know her daddy is a vicious, dangerous man. A convicted *criminal* in fact! And now – this awful man is molesting this innocent little girl!"

Bester Dumas sank back down into his chair, sounding like a sack of flour being dropped on the floor. He rubbed his clammy forehead with two skinny fingers, "Did Callie tell you her father had done something inappropriate?"

Marabell struck a theatrical pose and tilted her nose toward the ceiling. "Bester, I am a trained professional in these matters. You know I am a certified juvenile counselor and a founding member of the Summer County Parents to Stop Violence Against our Children. I *know* how to interpret this poor child's cry for help!" she retorted indignantly and tossed her short bleached hair for effect.

The principal leaned forward in his squeaky desk chair. "Tell me exactly what Callie said to you."

"Bester, she walked up to my desk in afternoon homeroom and looked me right in the eye." Dumas stared at the animated teacher for a long minute, waiting for her to continue. Finally, Marabell folded her arms and replied, "Callie said, 'Mrs. Jordan, if a man is doing something wrong to you, who should you tell?' And I said, 'You can tell me, Callie. You *should* tell me.' Then she said, 'I can't tell you. I can't tell anybody.' Then the bell rang and she scooted out before I could say anything else."

The principal pressed his thin lips tightly together and rubbed his forehead again. "So Callie didn't say it *was* her father or even exactly *what* is happening to her?"

"Oh, Bester Dumas! You know as well as I do that a molested child always talks in code. And it has to be her old daddy. Malachi Baines should have been in prison the last three years anyway. He maliciously cut a man's arm off!" Marabell put one hand on each side of her broad hips and strutted right up in Dumas' face. "Well, I of course *immediately* reported this heinous crime to J.P. and he's on his way out here right this minute."

Dumas backed away from the huffy teacher and nervously straightened his narrow tie. "Do you really think we need to involve the sheriff before we gather more complete information?"

"He *is* my husband and he *is* the sheriff of this county. He *has* to be involved," she pompously pronounced and tossed her head again.

When Dumas looked back toward the parking lot, he saw J.P. Jordan climbing out of his patrol car. In a few more minutes, the tall gray lawman politely knocked on the half-opened office door. "Come in, Sheriff," the principal called.

"Hello Bester," J.P. said as he shook Dumas' hand, then gently patted his wife on her shoulder. "Marabell tells me some very disturbing news about one of our young girls."

Dumas cleared his throat, "Uhh...well...yes, J.P. Based on what little information we have, it does indeed sound very disturbing."

The sheriff placed his hands on the desktop and leaned forward, staring out the window toward the departing school buses. "The sheriff's department will take over this

9

investigation, Bester. Let's try to keep this whole thing quiet around the school. You know how mean kids can be to each other. This little girl's already been through enough."

"Of course, Sheriff," Dumas agreed. "Don't you or someone in the department need to interview Callie here at school?"

J.P. pushed up and looked the smaller man in the eye. "Let us make those decisions, Bester. We'll interview whoever we think best, whenever we think best. Let's go home Marabell."

The teacher nodded approvingly toward her husband and, in her best patronizing tone said, "Yes Bester, it's always best to let the pros handle these kinds of delicate situations."

When the pair left his office, Bester slumped in his chair and contemplated all he had just heard. He, and almost everyone else in the county, had always trusted and respected J.P. Jordan. He did feel a sense of relief that a responsible adult would look into Callie's disturbing statement. At the same time, he felt apprehensive about the apparent rush to judgment and was still reeling from the sheriff's uncharacteristic abrupt response.

Chamblee Dam Road   *Summer County*   *May 19, 1998*

The midday sun had rapidly turned a brisk spring morning into a warm summer day. The broad-shouldered man smiled to himself as he hoisted the heavy cooler into the back of his green conservation department SUV. He had enjoyed a wonderful morning of fishing. As he had hoped, the stripe were running in the tailrace. His cooler was packed with striped bass fillets as well as pounds of fresh channel cat and largemouth.

Rocky Barnett swung his muscular body into the driver's seat and automatically reached to flip on his radios. *Nah*, he thought to himself. This was a rare off day. The Fish and Game Division *and* the Sheriff's Department could do without his services for at least one day. He would wait an hour or so more anyway before he checked in.

The patrol vehicle slowly headed north on the meandering gravel road leading back to Chamblee Dam. The husky game warden fumbled in his glove compartment and dug out a cigar – a very fine cigar – one he had been saving for a moment just such as this. He clipped the eight-inch Griffin with his pocketknife and slowly lit up. As he puffed out the sweet smoke, a feeling of euphoria swept over him. At this savored moment in time, Rocky Barnett's life was absolutely perfect.

Truthfully, at most moments in time, Rocky's life was near perfect. He thumped the first round of ashes out the window and pondered the direction his life was taking. Rocky knew he *could* have ended up in a lot of places. He had earned a degree in wildlife management. He had graduated from both the state police and the FBI academies. He had passed up lucrative offers to manage private hunting plantations. He had also considered several high school coaching jobs and even one college offer. He could have taken a position in a big city police department. A few years ago he looked like a lock for stardom in the NFL. But he was in none of those places. He was here in Summer County. Back in his hometown, working full-time as a game warden and part-time as a deputy sheriff. He liked it here. He liked his jobs. He liked his simple life.

The cigar eventually burned down to a stub. When Rocky turned onto county highway 87, he couldn't stand it any longer. Off day or not, he had to know if anything was happening. At 1:30 he radioed in to his game and fish enforcement command post. As expected, all was quiet on the home front. This was always a slow time of the year. A few minutes later he switched on the sheriff's department frequency. Within seconds, he heard that something exceptional was taking place in north Summer County.

"10-4, Eagle Eye, Alpha team one is positioned west of Forest Service Bridge, Alpha team two is still proceeding north on Ranger Station Road."

"What the hell!" Rocky said aloud as he reached for the mike. He knew immediately that the sheriff's department had deployed both its swat teams in a remote corner of the Cherokee National Forest. "Eagle Eye" meant J.P. had activated the department's level-one emergency response mode and was now directing the operation from a mobile command center. It required every deputy from every shift as well as every active reserve deputy for Summer County to man two eight-man swat teams. Rocky realized he was the only officer in the county not on this large scale mission.

"Officer R12 to base!" he shouted into the open mike.

"Go ahead R12. What's your 20 Rocky?"

"Proceeding north on 87 just south of Maple Cove – what's going down Rita Jo?"

"The department's in level one response with Alpha-Alpha."

"What's the situation?"

"Armed fugitives," the dispatcher replied tensely. "All other info radio blackout. Eagle Eye said if you called in to report to base code three."

"10-4. R12 en route code three." The blue lights flashed on top of the Tahoe. The piercing sound of the siren punctuated the honeysuckle-scented spring air. Rocky glanced at his dashboard as the speedometer registered past eighty. The young officer realized that in the growing afternoon heat his cool idyllic morning was fast becoming a memory.

TWO

Spud Jordan stopped and lifted his back foot out of the deep gluey mud. As the heavy combat boot pulled free, it made a loud sucking noise. Every step of the last one hundred yards had been a struggle in the dark, wet muck of Junee Bottoms. "Damn, it's hot," Spud exclaimed.

His partner, Billy Gentry, was breathing hard and trying to shift his heavy Kevlar vest to a more comfortable position. "Yeah," he agreed, "and we've still got a half-mile of this sticky shit."

Spud raised his radio toward his wet face. "Alpha-One leader to D-4."

Three hundred yards to Spud's right and hidden from his view by a massive tangle of blackberry and sweetgums, Deputy Hank Fincher keyed his mike and responded, "D-4 copies, Alpha-One. Uhh, what – "

At that moment, Fincher screamed with pain into his radio. The radio then went silent, but Jordan and Gentry could hear the sounds of a vicious melee across the thick tangle of brush. As they fought through the barrier of briars, Fincher's blood-curdling screams cut through the pungent marsh air again and again. Spud heard Fincher's partner, Charlie Dumas, shouting profanities then two quick shots rang out across the swamp bottom. Dumas went suddenly silent as Jordan and Gentry battled forward through the brambles. A mere fifty yards away they still could not see the scene, but were horrified by the sounds of crashing brush, splashing water and ferocious growls and snarls.

After what seemed an eternity, but was actually only seven minutes, Spud broke through the last wall of briars into a narrow boggy opening. He and Billy Gentry surged forward with weapons drawn and glimpsed a group of dark animals dashing away into the swamp's depths. The small grassy plot inside the thick morass was a grizzly scene. Ten feet away, reserve deputy Charlie Dumas lay disfigured in a swirl of bloody mud and leaves. Spud slowly turned his head to the left and felt a cold shock surge through his body. It appeared that Hank Fincher's torso had been torn into four or more pieces.

"Oh, dear God!" Gentry gasped and began to vomit uncontrollably.

Spud grabbed his radio and shouted, "Double zero! Double zero! Officers down!"

The remaining four deputies on Spud's Alpha-One team had been proceeding northeast across Junee Bottoms, roughly parallel to Fincher and Dumas, with Buck Yancey and Willie Gaddis being the closest pair. Lem Hawkins and Dave Ellis flanked them to their right. When Fincher began to scream, all four deputies charged to their left toward the sound.

Hawkins and Ellis caught up to the other two, but the four soon encountered the opposite side of the briar tangle that had impeded Spud and Billy Gentry. The four deputies were still struggling through the thorns when they heard the chilling "officer down" radio transmission. Approximately two minutes later, in the heart of a forty-acre mass of thorny barbs, the four were attacked without warning.

A large black animal sprang silently from the waist-high cover and sank his teeth into Deputy Hawkins' throat. The force of the charge knocked the officer into the blackberry vines and out of sight.

Dave Ellis, leading the way through the thicket, drew his handgun and stepped toward Hawkins' attacker. In the process he almost stepped on another large beast lying in ambush beneath the thick scrub. It appeared Ellis had tripped a landmine. The green underbrush erupted in an explosion of black hair and white fangs. The hidden brute grabbed on Ellis' groin and viciously shook his whole body.

Bloody chaos engulfed the swampy underbrush as at least four additional animals charged the deputies from the thicket. Spud Jordan and Billy Gentry heard a single piercing cry from the site of the second attack. Then all the deputies in the area heard a volley of shots that lasted several minutes. Dave Ellis apparently shot the animal that had latched onto his abdomen before he passed out from the pain. His weapon was found to be missing two rounds. Official police reports later concluded that during the next frantic minutes, Deputy Gaddis fired twelve rounds from his pistol while Buck Yancey discharged five shots from his shotgun and another five rounds from his 9mm Glock.

At 2:36 pm, Deputy Yancey sobbed plaintively into his radio, "10-double zero. 10-double zero. They're all down! They're all down!"

THREE

Rocky covered the last thirty miles north into town in less than twenty minutes. He listened in helpless shock to the horrifying radio communications from Spud's Alpha team. The stunned deputies near the scene were speculating that their comrades had fallen victim to attacks from a pack of wild boars or maybe coyotes. Rocky knew without doubt that neither theory was the case.

The blue jean-clad reserve deputy burst into the Sheriff's department Operation Center and was immediately struck by the eerily deserted appearance of the cavernous room. Only dispatcher Rita Jo Cook and the county's Emergency Management director, Chic Johnson, were present in the huge office. When Rita Jo saw Rocky come through the door, she removed her headphones and raced across the room to embrace him. Sobbing heavily, she gasped, "Oh, Rocky. It's bad. It's so bad. Hank ..." She was crying so hard she could not finish her sentence. "Hank ... and Charlie and Lem and Willie - They're all dead." She wailed out of control and squeezed his sweat-soaked tee shirt tightly. It was a full minute before she could speak again. "They don't know if Ellis is going to make it either. He's hurt real bad. They're still trying to stop Buck's bleeding."

"I know. I know. I have to get out there." He gently patted the back of her neck and said softly, "I need you to go back to your station Rita Jo."

The petite dispatcher nodded her head bravely and returned to her desk.

Chic Johnson walked over to Rocky and said in a shaky voice, "We've got four more ambulances ready to roll from town. J.P. wants you to escort 'em up there. We've already dispatched two ambulances and both EMT units. They'll be running about fifteen minutes ahead of you. A deputy's going to meet 'em at Rooster Bridge."

"Okay Chic. I'm on my way. Send 'em north on eighty-seven. I'll pick 'em up."

As he turned to leave, Chic added ominously, "The coroner is riding out with one of the ambulance service guys."

Associated Press wire service: Summer, Alabama 3:05 pm   May 19, 1998

> *Local news sources have reported that as many as four officers of the Summer County Sheriff's Department have been killed while conducting a raid in the Cherokee National Forest. Several other deputies were seriously injured. Sources have told the Associated Press that a sheriff's department SWAT team was attempting to search the isolated compound of a heavily armed family cult leader in connection with child molestation allegations. It is unclear at this point if the officers died from gunshot wounds.*

Cherokee National Forest, Summer County   6:45 pm   May 19, 1998

The orange fireball of the afternoon sun had begun a slow retreat to the horizon over the empty vastness of Junee Bottoms. Spud Jordan and Rocky Barnett had worked stoically side by side for the past two hours. The boyhood friends had assisted in the grim task of recovering and transporting the mangled bodies of four fellow officers from the unforgiving thicket tangles of the swamp bottom. When the ambulance carrying the last body rolled away down Ranger Station Road, Spud dropped to his knees on the chert roadbed in fatigue and despair.

Rocky knelt beside the chief deputy and said, "Spud. Look at me."

Spud raised his head and looked his oldest friend in the eye. Briar thorns had repeatedly ripped his face and dried blood caked his cheeks and forehead in several places.

"Why did J.P. send you all out here? He didn't even get a warrant! You've been trying to tell me he 'just wanted to talk' to Malachi about some hearsay allegation? You know damn well if J.P. wanted to talk to Malachi, all he had to do was send me up there by myself. Hell! I've brought him in for J.P. twice before, and three more times on Game and Fish business. I've never had a problem!" Rocky stood and yanked Spud up by his bloodstained shirtfront. Shaking his exhausted friend like a rag doll, he shouted angrily in his face. "This didn't have to happen! J.P. was asking for trouble – charging up there like the damn cavalry! Four good men died because of this macho bullshit!" He released Spud's collar and the gangly deputy collapsed back onto the gravel road.

Spud weakly raised his head. "I don't know Rock. I work for the man just like you do. Being his nephew don't make me special. He's the boss. I've always followed his orders and so have you." They were both silent for a long moment. "There's no way J.P. could've known ahead of time about these half-breed coyotes or whatever they are."

"Damn it! Damn it! Damn it, Spud! Those weren't coyotes! It's a pack of wild dogs that's been in this same area for years! I've always known about them! If J.P. had told me what he was planning, I would've warned him!"

"Look, Rock. It was your off day. J.P. probably thought he couldn't wait for you. He …."

"Bullshit! That's just pure bullshit! You know damn well he could have waited one more day. He caused these guys to die! Our guys, Spud. Our guys! Our friends."

Spud covered his face with his battered hands and started crying. "I know, Rock. I saw it all," he sobbed. "You're gonna have to ask J.P. about it yourself."

Associated Press wire service: Summer, Alabama   5:15 pm   May 19, 1998

A spokesman for the Summer County Emergency Management Agency has confirmed that four sheriff's deputies were killed around 2:30 pm, central time, in the Cherokee National Forest. Two other officers have been hospitalized, one in critical condition. All six deputies were members of a special sheriff's department SWAT team attempting to search the remote encampment of cult leader Malachi Baines. Baines, who has a criminal record, was wanted for questioning in connection with child molestation allegations. Preliminary reports from the scene indicate that the slain officers may have been mauled to death by large guard dogs near the Baines family compound.

Cherokee National Forest, Summer County   8:00 pm   May 19, 1998

Rocky zipped up the heavy Carhartt jacket. The instant warmth of the thick garment felt good in the cooling night air over his sweat-soaked underclothes. He flipped the switch on the battery pack and adjusted the powerful headlamp attached to his hard hat. He chambered a shell into his 3 ½ -inch magnum Benelli and turned to face the headlights from the patrol car easing up the road beside him. Deputy Sam Gibson rolled down his window. "Rocky you going back in there *tonight*?"

"Yeah Sam. I'm going to trail up those dead dogs and drag 'em out. There may be a few that need to be finished off. There's blood trails leading out in every direction."

"Good gosh, nobody in their right mind would go out in the dark after those killers by their self!"

"It's no big deal Sam. I'm used to working by myself at night."

The middle-aged deputy hesitated, then turned off his engine and opened his door. "I'll go with you Rocky."

The game warden walked up and closed the door on the cruiser. "I appreciate the offer Sam, but I don't really need any help. You guys've been through a living hell today. Go on home."

"I'm the last man out, Rocky. You'll be in there with no backup."

"It's okay Sam. I'll really be just fine."

Gibson finally relented and Rocky watched his tail lights disappear down Ranger Station Road. When Gibson's car was out of sight, Rocky turned and followed the beam of his powerful light down what was now a well-defined path into the boggy thicket. He had walked a little over four hundred yards when his beam highlighted the yellow ribbons of crime scene tape draped around the tops of broken brush tangles. The tape marked the spot where Lem Hawkins and Willie Gaddis had died less than six hours earlier. Rocky paused and stared at the tape, thinking that in the middle of a Junee Bottoms briar patch, a crime scene marker appeared strikingly out of place.

He swept his head left to right in a slow arc. Under the beam of light, the sea of bright white blackberry blooms reminded him of fresh snow cover. Over his right shoulder, a whippoorwill started calling out in the night melody of its repetitious whistle. The deep woods were stirring with the sounds of summer night life.

The sights and sounds of the dark forest were of great comfort to Rocky Barnett. He was truly in his natural element. He had never been afraid in the night woods. From the beginning of his career as a game warden, he had pursued and arrested armed night poachers without a second thought. He was neither unaware nor consumed by the obvious dangers. It was simply a basic part of his job. He felt a myriad of emotions standing in the middle of Junee Bottoms this cool May night, but fear was not among them.

Rocky stepped forward inside the police tape and stood in the very spot where Lem Hawkins' throat had been crushed. He felt a wave of grief and empathy for his lost friend. He could only imagine the terror that Lem must have felt in his final ghastly seconds of life.

Five years ago, a wild dog just a few miles from this spot had aggressively attacked Rocky. He had quickly shot the animal loose from his leg but would never forget the shock of the surprise attack. The ten-inch scar on his left calf suddenly seemed very insignificant.

Over the next two hours Rocky located, tagged, and pulled five dead dogs out to the road. Two of the large canines were shot dead inside the taped-off crime scene. Two more had been wounded and bled to death several hundred feet into the brush. A fifth dog apparently had its spine severed by a buckshot pellet and had dragged himself away over three hundred yards into the swamp. Rocky methodically trailed the severely injured animal until he located it lying against the base of an old cypress stump. When the headlight beam glared in the black dog's amber eyes, it uttered a deep threatening growl. Without panic or passion, the game warden calmly fired a nine-millimeter round into its neck and proceeded to drag the limp carcass back out to his vehicle.

Associated Press wire service: Summer, Alabama   8:25 pm   May 19, 1998

Summer County Sheriff, J.P. Jordan, has confirmed that four of his deputies were mauled to death earlier today by a pack of large attack dogs. A fifth deputy was severely maimed and has been air lifted to Birmingham's University Hospital where he remains in critical condition. Sergeant Hank Fincher, Sergeant Lem Hawkins, Deputy Willie Gaddis and Reserve Deputy Charlie Dumas were all killed between 2:15 pm and 2:30 pm central time. Reserve Deputy Dave Ellis and Deputy Earlon "Buck" Yancey were also injured in the incident. Sheriff Jordan indicated that his deputies were attacked while attempting to question cultist Malachi Baines regarding child molestation allegations. Baines has a lengthy criminal record and is a well-known figure to the sheriff's department. The sheriff believes that the dogs belong to the Baines family and have been trained to guard the remote family compound from intruders. Jordan stated his intentions to seek murder indictments against Malachi Baines and certain other members of his family.

Summer, Alabama   9:15 pm   May 19, 1998

J.P. Jordan lumbered across the room and collapsed his large frame into the padded recliner. He felt as if every ounce of energy was drained from his body. It had required all of the sixty-four year old lawman's focus to complete the emotional press conference. Marabell had finally taken enough "nerve medicine" to knock herself out and he could hear her snoring loudly in the adjacent bedroom. He was finally alone with his thoughts for the first time since the tragedy had struck. In the quiet intimacy of his small den, there were images he could not escape. Earlier in the evening he had taken the time to visit individually with the families of his slain deputies. J.P. could still vividly see the confused pain in the faces of their wives and children. He felt a searing agony deep in his soul.

The ringing of the telephone shattered his brief moments of reflection. He picked up the receiver and heard a familiar voice.

"J.P. I've been trying to call you all evening!"

"Hello, Governor. I've been expecting you to call."

"Gosh my friend, you knew I would. I know you've been busy with the families and the press conference so we've been working behind the scenes to mobilize some help for you. I'll be in Summer in the morning standing beside you."

Governor Bog Allen's hometown of Pineville was just thirty miles away in adjoining Chalk County. The governor and the sheriff went back a long way together.

"Okay. Thanks Bog. I knew we could count on you."

"Look, J.P. I don't know what you had in mind from the state. Nothing like this has ever happened up there before. But I've taken the liberty of asking the Alabama Bureau of Investigation to look into your officers' deaths. The Attorney General has called to say if you have any problem with your local DA going after murder indictments, he will gladly prosecute the case himself. And I'm sending you a couple dozen troopers to help seal off the hideout. If we have to, we'll call in the National Guard to smoke the bastard out!"

J.P. listened quietly before responding. "That's ah … that's all good Bog." In his tired mind the grieving sheriff saw the investigation mushrooming out of his control.

When the conversation was finished, J.P. hung up the phone and slumped back into his easy chair. He scanned the photo-covered wall that faced him. His blood-shot eyes fixed onto the black-and-white picture of his dad. In a photograph labeled 1958, the stone-faced John Powell Jordan, Sr. stood on the steps of the "new" sheriff's office in Summer. The old man had been a legendary Summer County sheriff in the forties and fifties. J.P. had now walked in his father's large footsteps for thirty-six years. In all those years, a Summer deputy had never been killed in the line of duty. In fact, until 2:15 today, no officer had ever died on duty in the entire history of the department. In the haze of reliving his surreal day, the sheriff still could not accept the macabre loss of four men.

A little after 10:30 the phone rang again. J.P. was almost too drained to answer. County coroner Jake Looney was on the other end of the line. "I hate to bother you at this time of night J.P., but I've discovered something you need to know. Willie Gaddis did not die from dog bites." When the sheriff did not respond, Looney continued, "He was chewed up pretty bad on his arms and legs – but the cause of death was a gunshot wound to the chest."

J.P. finally spoke, "Was it a round from a hunting rifle?"

"No, sheriff. Unfortunately I believe it was a nine millimeter handgun slug fired from close range."

J.P. exhaled a long deep sigh. "Jesus Christ, Jake. This nightmare just keeps getting worse."

FOUR

Rocky waited for the coffeemaker to utter its last gurgle and poured his first steaming cup of the new day. It had been a short night. He had delivered the dog carcasses to Stanley Wilson's vet office around 11:30 and returned to his lakeside cabin well after midnight. Rocky walked with his coffee mug to the big front window and gazed out over fog-shrouded Lake Chamblee. The lights down at Dye's Landing Marina emitted a fuzzy yellow glow through the thin patches of pre-dawn mist. Bo padded up and inserted his broad head under Rocky's dangling left hand and whined pleadingly for attention. He stroked the old lab's graying nose. "We've got ourselves a little fog out this morning old buddy." Bo slowly wagged his thick tail as if agreeing with his master's weather pronouncement.

Turning back into the rustic wood-paneled main room, Rocky picked up the remote and clicked on the television set. He typically watched national news once a day, usually around 4:00 a.m. The big screen mounted on the wall beside the rock fireplace flickered to life and instantly galvanized Rocky's attention. The CNN reporter was talking about the deaths in Summer County. The large block caption at the bottom of the screen read "Deputy Mauling Murders." The anchorman, with great drama in his voice,

26

said, "The bloody standoff with local police continues near Tate's Gap in north central Alabama's Cherokee National Forest. A heavily armed family militia led by convicted felon Malachi Baines continues to hold dozens of county and state police at bay. The Baines enclave is situated atop a mountain ridge of private land known as Piney Bald, which is encircled by the 200,000 acre Cherokee National Forest. Reports now indicate that Summer County officials, with the help of Alabama state troopers, have surrounded and sealed off the Baines compound."

Rocky spoke out loud to his canine companion lying quietly at his feet. "Surrounded? It would take the *Third Infantry Division* a month to *surround* Piney Bald! They probably have a trooper car turned sideways across Tate's Gap Road and call that *sealed off*!" Bo thumped his tail a few times on the heart pine floor to indicate he agreed the news report was absurd.

The commentator continued, "The armed stalemate in the Alabama mountains is reminiscent of the 1992 Idaho siege by federal agents at Ruby Ridge. In both incidents, trained attack dogs were unleashed on officers attempting to apprehend an entrenched suspect. However, the horrific mauling murders of four Alabama deputies exceeds any previous dog attacks in U.S. history."

Rocky slammed his heavy mug down on the table top. "Gosh Bo, our guys were not *murdered*! They died in a wild animal attack. Malachi Baines has nothing to do with the damn feral dogs!" He stood and headed toward the shower. "Bo, I've got to talk to J.P."

Approaching the outskirts of town, Rocky squirmed and twisted in the discomfort of his starched polyester deputy's uniform. It was Wednesday, so he was a Summer County deputy sheriff for at least one full shift. On Wednesdays and Thursdays he always dreaded exchanging the functional comfort of his game warden fatigues for the stiff tan deputy garb.

As he drove into the courthouse square he noticed an amazing frenzy of activity. He saw a half-dozen satellite news trucks scattered around the square. He noted channel logos from Birmingham and Montgomery as well as CNN and Fox News vehicles. The sheriff's office parking lot was crowded with state highway patrol cars and five troopers chatted in a cluster on the back sidewalk. Rocky knew from his radio transmissions that the troopers had established a mobile command post at Tate's Gap and that ABI agents had been dispatched to the site of the attacks in Junee Bottoms. When he climbed out of the Tahoe, he could see that J.P.'s cruiser was already parked in its reserved spot. As Rocky approached the rear entrance, a trooper he had never seen before pushed open the heavy door for him and patted his back as he entered.

The sheriff's office was as crowded as the courthouse square. Thirty or forty strangers sat on desks or talked in small groups. There were more state troopers, ABI agents in their identification windbreakers, several deputies from Chalk County and at least a dozen guys in suits. Most of the suits looked like investigators or agents of some kind. Frank Lipscomb, the Summer County day shift sergeant, pushed through the crowd and embraced Rocky with his huge hairy arms. "Hey man, I didn't get to see you yesterday, but I heard you worked all afternoon and half the night. I wish you could've been out there with Spud's team. You know that area better than any of us."

Rocky returned the hearty pats. "Yeah, Lip. You just don't know how much I wish I could've been with you guys."

The round-faced sergeant released his embrace. "Rocky, I'm having our morning roll call in the coffee room. If everybody's in, we might get started in about ten minutes. It's gonna be one helluva long day."

"Yeah, okay. But I've got to see J.P. first."

"Rocky I need your help as soon as possible. You're the only man I've got who can show these state agents what they need to see up in Junee Bottoms."

"I'm sorry Lip – but this can't wait." Rocky turned and walked over to the sheriff's private office door. As he tapped on the glass window, he could see the boss had a telephone cradled against his ear. J.P. looked up and motioned for him to enter. As he entered the paneled room, Rocky heard the sheriff say soberly, "Okay Jake. But we're not going public with this until the press conference," before he hung up the phone.

Rocky approached the sheriff's desk and wondered if J.P. could already see the anger on his face. It was immediately obvious that the sheriff was too absorbed in his own thoughts to notice anything.

"Sit down son," the older man said with a faraway look in his faded blue eyes. "I've got more bad news. You'll be the first to know. I haven't even told Spud." J.P. turned his gaze onto Rocky's tanned face and said without emotion, "Willie was not killed by the dogs. He was shot through the heart. It was a 9mm slug at close range.

Since Lem carried a .40 caliber that wasn't even fired, the shot had to come from Willie's own weapon or Ellis' or Buck's. Jake has asked the state lab to run the ballistics tests."

The news was so stunning that Rocky's animosity briefly subsided. "Was Willie not wearing his vest?"

"No. When they started running toward Hank, Buck remembers suggesting that they both shuck the helmets and the Kevlar. Buck apparently kept his on but Willie dropped his about two hundred yards from the attack." J.P. paused and looked out the glass-front door toward the crowd of officers milling around. "I'll be giving this information to the reporters later this morning."

Both men sat silently. Rocky stared into J.P.'s wrinkled face. He looked very old and very tired. Rocky felt a surge of compassion for his longtime mentor but could no longer hold back his tidal wave of emotions. "J.P. nothing about this sounds right to me. You know I could've brought Malachi in by myself! You could've waited another half day. And the whole allegation seems extremely suspect. Malachi Baines is capable of doing a lot of things. *Nobody* understands that better than I do. In certain situations he can be a dangerous man. But I'll never believe he raped his daughter. That runs contrary to everything he's about."

The sheriff remained stoic. "I had credible evidence. Marabell heard the girl's story firsthand and I decided that the child shouldn't be exposed to that abuse for even another single day."

"She's your wife, sheriff. But I know Malachi and his family better than anyone in this county and I don't believe Callie was implicating her father."

J.P. didn't respond and Rocky continued with a rising tension in his voice. "But regardless of all that – sheriff, you've got to stop this nonsense talk about murder charges! That pack of dogs has run wild in Junee Bottoms for over ten years. They probably trace back to hog dogs that the Grant brothers let loose up there in the late-80s. I had a dog attack near there myself! Malachi doesn't *own* those feral dogs! Nobody does. They are wild animals! Hell, their normal range doesn't even come close to Piney Bald. The Baines' would shoot them on sight if they got anywhere near their hunting dogs." Rocky stood up red faced and glared at his silver-haired boss. "The news reports say you're asking for murder indictments. Is that true J.P.?"

The veteran lawman remained composed in the heat of his deputy's outburst. "Take your seat son," he said quietly. "This thing has gotten a lot bigger than you or me. A lot bigger than just Summer County. The state's already jumped in with both feet. Last night I learned that the feds have an interest in the case. Junee Bottoms is in the national forest. The attacks happened on U.S. government property. The ATF wants to start with a weapons warrant and go from there." He gestured with his right hand toward the outer office. "We already have the FBI and the U.S. Marshals sitting out there drinking our coffee. This whole damn thing is spiraling out of my control. If the Summer County DA doesn't produce a murder indictment, then the state attorney general will and probably the U.S. attorney won't be far behind."

Rocky sat back down without speaking. The sheriff slowly rubbed his broad chin and looked his godson in the eye. "Rock, I've known you since you were a baby. You've always been like my own. You and Spud are the closest thing I'll ever have to sons. You've made yourself into a fine man and one helluva good officer – maybe the best I've ever seen. You have good instincts for police work and you make good judgments. I trust your judgment." A look of deep sadness crossed the old man's face. "I've made some mistakes and it cost a big price. A lot of what you just said about this case may be true. But I couldn't stop the indictments against Malachi Baines now, even if I wanted to – and I'm not sure I do. He'll get his day in court, but he's going to be indicted for murder Rock, and neither of us can change that."

Rocky stood again and started pacing. "He could never be convicted. There is no way any prosecutor will ever prove he owns those dogs. It's a waste of everybody's time and it's just plain *wrong*! If we can put a lid on this murder rubbish, maybe I can find out what's *really* been going on with Callie."

The sheriff stood and leaned forward toward Rocky, placing both hands on his desktop. "At this point, that would be nothing but a waste of *your* time. I believe Baines is molesting his little girl. I know you don't agree. Maybe we can sort it out later. But right now, I need your help son. I need you to coordinate the requests for crime scene visits with all these federal and state guys. And aah, sometime soon I can tell you there will be another trip up to Piney Bald - this time with arrest warrants. I know you have arrested Baines five times by yourself, so I will do everything I can to see that you are the point man when the time comes."

Rocky stopped pacing and crossed his arms. "In his own way, Malachi Baines is a fair man. When I arrested him for assaulting Slick Hines, he *knew* he had done it and *I* knew he had done it. We had an honest understanding. All that was left to talk about was when and how he was coming in. This is different. He and I both know he didn't have a damn thing to do with the dog attacks and probably nothing to do with Callie's story. In Malachi's mind, surrendering on a bogus murder charge would be a fool's game. He'll see it for the poisoned trap it is." Rocky's voice got softer and he placed a hand on the sheriff's shoulder. "Please listen to me J.P. Take a good hard look before you back a murder indictment. The evidence is just not there and nobody – not me, not you – not a hundred federal agents will ever arrest Malachi on a murder rap without a fight. Everything's already bad enough J.P. Please don't let more good men die because of this phony charge."

The sheriff was visibly shaken by his protégé's pleas. He sat back down and rubbed his chin again. His eyes moistened. "Son, you're a good man. A better man than I am. But, I can't make you any promises." The old sheriff rose and embraced the young deputy in a long bear hug.

FIVE

A large but subdued local crowd and over seventy reporters assembled on the fresh-cut grass in front of the ancient building. Summer, Alabama was a very old town and its august courthouse had been center stage for many historic moments. Summer was the state's first capital and in 1819 the inaugural Alabama legislature convened on the antiquated structure's second floor. In 1861, Robert E. Lee spent a day inside the building debating the merits of armed insurrection with Harlan B. Summer before the two reluctant warriors finally conceded the inevitable. In 1969 President Richard Nixon stood on the broad courthouse steps to award the Congressional Medal of Honor posthumously to local Vietnam War hero Peter Hawkins. However, no event had ever focused more widespread attention on the time-honored courthouse square than the grotesque deaths of four deputies.

A row of microphones was clustered on the top step when Sheriff J.P. Jordan and Governor Bog Allen walked out the front door to begin a press conference covered by every network and cable outlet. The sheriff went first and somberly read a prepared statement in his distinctive throaty voice. "Yesterday, near the Tate's Gap community, four Summer County deputies died in the line of duty. A fifth deputy was critically

34

injured and is fighting for his life in a Birmingham hospital. A sixth deputy remains hospitalized at Summer County Regional Hospital in serious but stable condition. These deaths and injuries to our officers were the result of attacks from dogs believed to belong to suspects currently under investigation. The death of Deputy Willie Gaddis resulted from a single gunshot wound. An investigation is currently under way to determine the source of the fatal shot. The attacks occurred inside the boundaries of the Cherokee National Forest. Therefore, as of today, federal officials are joining state and Summer County officials in the investigation of this incident. County, state and federal officers have jointly sealed off the home of Malachi Baines which is in an area known as Piney Bald. The next steps taken by law enforcement will be determined by the outcome of the investigations into the deaths of our officers and the degree of cooperation offered by Malachi Baines." J.P. looked up from his text and continued, "Governor Bog Allen has long been a good friend to the citizens of Summer County. We appreciate the governor being here today to support and assist our efforts. After the governor speaks, we will try to answer your questions. Governor."

Allen stepped forward and began his animated speech without referring to any notes. "Thank you, sheriff. We are all saddened by the loss of four brave men. Four brave men who gave their lives to serve and protect Summer County. Four brave men who were leaders and positive examples in their community. Our first concern is for the families of these fallen heroes. My office is doing everything possible to comfort these good people in their time of great sorrow. We are providing grief counselors and financial assistance. This morning I instructed the state finance director to expedite the payment of life insurance proceeds to the families. These checks will in fact be issued

35

and hand-delivered today. Since reserve deputies are not included in the state employee benefits programs, the governor's office will use emergency discretionary funds to provide an immediate stipend to the families of deputies Charlie Dumas and Dave Ellis."

The governor's face hardened as he stared into the cameras. Shaking a closed fist, he thundered, "And I can assure all the fine people of Summer County that justice will be done in this appalling tragedy. If certain individuals are responsible for these senseless deaths, we will use every resource available to apprehend and arrest them! And we *will* prosecute them to the full extent of the law!"

When the governor finished speaking and stepped back, a collective murmur arose from the large gaggle of reporters and hands shot up from every direction. J.P. pointed toward a short woman near the front and the CNN correspondent said, "Sheriff, you just stated that deputy Gaddis was shot to death. Does that mean someone in the Baines compound fired the shot and if not, who did fire the shot?"

J.P. responded calmly, "We are investigating the source of the shot. When that investigation is complete, we will announce the findings."

The woman shouted again in her shrill voice, "A follow up, Sheriff. Could one of your deputies have fired the fatal shot?"

"I will not speculate about that until we complete our investigation."

The sheriff pointed toward another reporter. "Governor, it seems obvious from your comments that you believe the attacks should be treated as homicides. Is there any possibility that Malachi Baines was *not* responsible for the incident?"

The governor assumed his most serious countenance. "We have not concluded our investigation. If it *is* determined that Mr. Baines, or anyone else, is responsible for these tragic deaths, then I assure you they *will* be pursued to the full extent of the law."

"But Governor," the reporter persisted, "it sounds like a stretch to assume that anyone necessarily owned or controlled the dogs. Isn't it true that the Baines family lives more than a mile from the site of the attack and no one else lives closer than at least five miles?"

Allen replied, "The sheriff is in a better position to know the details of who lives in the area. J.P. would you like to respond?"

For the first time, J.P. looked uncomfortable. He cleared his throat and said, "The attacks occurred in a section of the national forest known as Junee Bottoms. Malachi Baines and his family own the closest residence to the site. There are no other homes in the immediate area."

The sheriff pointed in another direction and a tall ABC reporter said, "Going back to Jim's question, how far was the attack from the Baines home and I have a follow-up."

The sheriff was beginning to appear defensive. "The attack was approximately one mile from the Baines home," he replied curtly.

"Sheriff Jordan, then please explain to us exactly how Mr. Baines allegedly transported his attack dogs to the heavily wooded site and unleashed them on the deputies."

J.P. struggled to regain his composure. "We have not alleged that Mr. Baines *is* responsible for the attacks. What we have said is that it is very probable that *someone* is responsible for the attacks and that Mr. Baines is certainly a suspect. We will wait for the outcome of our investigation before we say more."

A reporter in the very back shouted, "Sheriff, I understand that several of the dogs were killed and are being examined by state veterinarians. What kind of dogs were these and did they have collars or any other identification?"

J.P. answered, "They are large cross breeds. Most of the ones we recovered weighed over one hundred pounds. Even as much as one hundred fifty. I guess they appear to be Rottweiler or pit bull crosses. We will have more information about the dogs once they have been examined."

"And any collars, Sheriff?"

"The five we killed and recovered were not wearing collars."

An older male reporter shouted down his competitors to get the sheriff's attention. "Sheriff! Sheriff – can you tell us why your deputies, wearing full assault gear, were positioned in a forest area over a mile from their destination *and* if you had a warrant to search the Baines home?"

J.P.'s face was now full of stress lines as he gave his carefully measured answer. "We did not have a search warrant because we did not need a search warrant. Our intentions were not to *search* the home but rather to question Mr. Baines. Our objective was to convince the suspect to go back into town with us and answer some questions. Mr. Baines has a long history of violent confrontations. We were in our SWAT team gear to protect our people." The sheriff paused and glanced around the crowd. "There is no easy way to approach the Baines home. There is only one narrow road from Tate's Gap to their property. It crosses a high private bridge they have been known to sabotage.

38

The most secure approach to the Baines home is through the national forest. That is exactly what our deputies were attempting when they were attacked."

A local Birmingham reporter was finally recognized. "Sheriff Jordan," the young black woman began, "the initial concern was Mr. Baines' alleged molestation of his daughter. It is my understanding that across Alabama, in similar situations, the state Department of Human Resources is usually involved. Caseworkers are empowered to remove an endangered child on the spot and place the child in protective custody. DHR often works such cases accompanied by local police. Why did you not contact DHR and instead take an extremely heavy-handed approach with SWAT teams?"

The sheriff scowled. "We knew from long experience who we were dealing with. These are not the kind of people who just open their door and let a social worker waltz in!"

The governor finally relieved the sheriff from the rugged media grilling by announcing they had to get back to the investigation and other pressing matters. As the two speakers re-entered the courthouse, a dual buzz erupted over the courthouse grounds. For the assembled reporters, an already puzzling story was rapidly sprouting new loose ends. The several hundred townspeople however, felt a collective anger toward the media's skeptical line of questioning. No one in Summer had any trouble believing Malachi Baines raped his daughter or set his dogs loose on the deputies. The mountain families around Tate's Gap were widely viewed as crude and brutal clans.

As Rocky walked past the front row of booths, he was greeted at every table. Most of the men and boys shook his hand and two older women rose and hugged his neck. All the patrons in the Blue Bull restaurant knew Rocky and he knew them. Tonight, everyone in the place wanted to give a hometown hero his or her personal condolences. Like one large family, the town and the county were reeling from the shocking tragedy in Junee Bottoms. They were also universally rallying around their longtime sheriff and his department.

The popular deputy finally worked his way across the dining room and slipped into an empty booth in the back corner near the kitchen. He was still adjusting his tired body onto the worn vinyl seat when Skeeter Yates popped out from behind the counter and wiggled into the bench facing him. Skeeter and Rocky had been sweethearts in the first grade and "off and on" over the thirty years since. The "offs" usually came whenever Skeeter made another bad decision about a future ex-husband. These days, the two were rarely seen together outside of the Blue Bull, but local opinion still considered her the closest thing he had to a regular girlfriend.

"It's Wednesday so I've ordered you the beans and greens special," she announced in a singsong voice.

Rocky bowed his head and stroked his short-cropped blonde hair. "Thanks, Skeet. I'm really hungry. It's been a tough day."

"Oh, I bet it has. I know you gotta be real upset. This's all just so awful. I still can't believe it really happened. Do yah want me to go in the back and just be a good waitress or do yah need some talk-it-out therapy?"

He raised his head and looked into her warm brown eyes. He knew the options were offered in complete sincerity. That was one of Skeeter's most endearing qualities. She always gave him as much attention or as much space as he wanted. A tired smile crossed his handsome face. "I guess I *would* like to tell you what's heavy on my mind."

"Okay, Rock. I'm all yours." As another waitress, laden with four dinner platters scooted by, Skeeter called out, "Sally, tell George to clock me out."

Over two plates of turnip greens, pintos and cornbread, Rocky worked through his emotional burdens with the girl he had known for as long as he could remember.

Associated Press wire service: Summer, Alabama   8:45 pm   May 20, 1998

The AP has learned that ballistics tests confirm a bullet fired from the gun of Summer County deputy Earlon "Buck" Yancey took the life of fellow deputy Willie Gaddis. The shooting occurred Tuesday while Yancey, Gaddis and four other officers were being attacked by large dogs on a SWAT team raid in the Cherokee National Forest. Deputy Gaddis was the only black officer on the Summer County force and was the first African-American ever hired by the department. Local sources indicate that Yancey, who is white, and Gaddis were involved in a long-standing feud with often blatant racial overtones. The Summer County sheriff's department declined to confirm that Yancey had publicly threatened to kill Gaddis.

SIX

Veteran Newslink reporter Ted Logan walked into the office of the editor-in-chief and removed his sunshades. Susan Rollins smiled at the tall man with a three-day stubble. "Have a seat Ted. How about some coffee?"

"Okay, Susan. I'm still about five cups short today."

The silver-haired editor filled two cups from a pewter carafe and handed one to Logan. "Ted, this dog attack standoff down in Alabama is becoming a huge story. I want you to cover it."

Logan drank from his steaming cup and looked at his boss. Her strong ebony face was beginning to show the wear of 40 years in the publishing wars. "Yeah. Four dead deputies, maybe five. It's already bloodier than Ruby Ridge."

"Yes, it is. And it contains many of the same elements – plus this dog angle is freakish. Ruby Ridge was some of your best work. I have no doubt you will do this story justice."

Logan rested his coffee cup on the knee of his faded khaki slacks. "When do I leave?"

"As soon as possible."

"I'll need a couple hours to dig out all my grits recipes."

Susan smiled. "You know I was born and raised in Mississippi. I will loan you my mother's cookbook. You can thank me later for the cholesterol." Her dark penetrating eyes locked on his face. "And Mr. Logan...don't call home until you find out what's really going on down there."

Summer, Alabama   *2:30 pm*   *May 21, 1998*

Ted Logan slowly eased his rental car into the empty parking lot. He looked at the glass front door and noticed the "open" sign. A few minutes later he walked into the Blue Bull Restaurant, still not sure the place was really open. *Last remodeled when Truman was president*, he mused. He crossed the deserted dining room and plopped his six-foot-four frame down on a bar stool at the counter. The old stool made a loud squeak and a woman appeared from around a corner to his right. *"Whoa,"* he muttered, *"now that's a Dixie darling."* He slowly removed his sunglasses and looked the shapely brunette over from head to toe.

"You wanna menu?" the dark-eyed waitress asked.

"Oh, I don't know. Do I need one?"

"We-e-l-l-l, that depends on if yah know what yah want."

He smiled and the perky waitress smiled back. "Do I need a menu to order a cup of coffee?"

"No sir, you do not. I was just fixin' to start a fresh pot if yah wanna wait a few minutes."

"Great. I'll wait. Is this a no-smoking facility?"

"Absolutely not. George says as long as people pay to eat here they most certainly can smoke here too." She reached under the counter and produced a battered metal Marlboro ashtray. He dug out a cigarette and lit it with a paper-stemmed match. She watched his every move as he exhaled a plume of smoke toward the ceiling. "You're not from around here, are yah?"

He grinned. "Now what makes you say that?"

"If you were from here, I'd know who yah were!"

Ted studied her pretty face. She wore little makeup except for a faint pink color on her delicate lips. She had a fresh-scrubbed, girl-next-door look about her. "So that means you *are* from around here."

"Yep. Since the day I was born."

He thumped his ashes. "So what's your name?"

"Skeeter Yates."

"Is Skeeter what your friends call you or do you go by a nickname when you're off duty?"

She put her hands on her hips and stepped back from the counter. "Are you tryin' to be cute about my name?"

"When I'm talking to an attractive woman I never try to be cute."

She glared at him over her shoulder as she turned to get his coffee. As she walked away, he noticed she had a mass of shiny brown hair neatly piled on top of her head and held in place with a long barrette.

Skeeter sat the light green ceramic cup down in front of him. "Are you in town 'cause of the deputies gettin' killed?"

He lifted the thick cup. "Yeah, I am."

"You ain't a reporter, are yah?"

"Would it be a bad thing if I were?"

"No. I don't reckon it's a bad thing …. but you don't act like any reporter I've ever seen."

"Well Skeeter, I've worked hard for a long time to be different. Do you know much about the circumstances of the deputies' deaths?"

"Oh, yeah. It's so sad. I guess I know all 'bout it. Rocky's told me just 'bout everything that's happened."

"Who is Rocky?"

"Rocky Barnett! He's just probably the most important policeman in Summer County, besides maybe J.P. Who are *you*, anyway?"

"I'm Ted Logan. I write for Newslink. Tell me why Rocky is so important in Summer County."

She got a glimmer in her big brown eyes. "Well, Rocky's *always* been a big deal around here. He was a high school All-American! Led Summer to two straight state championships. It would've been three straight in '80 'cept for Cleo King dropping a pass in the end zone. Now that was some game. It was the state final. Rocky broke his left arm in the first quarter and still played the whole darn game! Gained two hundred yards and scored three touchdowns. On the last play, Spud hit Cleo right on the numbers at the goal line. Folks around here ain't never gonna forgive Cleo. Everbody says Rocky played his guts out with just one arm and Cleo just choked it for the whole town."

Logan raised his eyebrows. "You've just amazed me. I've never actually met a woman who really understood football."

"Oh, that's nothin'. If you live in Summer County, you talk football. Rocky would've been big time in the pros. He signed with Auburn. Made All-SEC his first year and All-American the next. His third year, he busted a knee over at Georgia. They never got it fixed where he could play again."

He lit another cigarette and looked at her. "You know a lot about his football career. Is Rocky your guy?"

Skeeter blushed. "Oh, I don't know 'bout that. He took me to the prom three years in a row and I've scrambled his eggs a lotta mornings ... but Rocky's not the marrying kind or anything like that. But ... I reckon I'd do most anything for him. You wanna refill?"

"Yeah, sure. So I assume Rocky is with the Sheriff's department?"

"He sure is. He's the county game warden *and* a deputy." She poured his cup to the rim again.

"What does Rocky think about the standoff with this wacko cult?"

"*What* did you say? They ain't no cult or no standoff! Rocky knows Malachi ain't got nothin' to do with those dogs."

"Malachi Baines? Doesn't he have a long criminal history?"

"Well no. Not really, I guess."

"I thought he was convicted for cutting off a man's arm."

46

She swatted her hand toward his face. "Goodness, no. Slick started that fight and three of those Hines boys was holdin' Malachi down over at the feed store. He just stuck Slick's arm with his pocketknife to make 'im turn loose. The doctors had to cut off his arm 'bout a month later 'cause it got infected."

"Do you think he is a dangerous man?"

"I don't guess. Rocky brings 'im in by hisself 'bout once a year."

"Why does he get arrested so often?"

"Oh, it's just little stuff. Mostly shooting deer in the summer time or trapping turkeys. Little stuff like that."

"Do you think you could arrange for me to talk with Rocky?"

Skeeter hesitated. "Maybe. Maybe so. I lay his supper out right here most ever night. I can see what he says."

"Okay. I would appreciate that. Could I stop here again tomorrow and talk to you?"

"Oh sure. I got plenty of time six days a week between dinner and supper." Ted stood and handed her a five-dollar bill. "Do yah want your change or do yah want to impress me?"

He smiled and walked out of the empty restaurant.

Summer County Courthouse   *4:00 pm*   *May 21, 1998*

For the second time in two days, a crowd was gathering below a cluster of microphones on the old building's front steps. The townspeople milling around in the

47

afternoon heat were buzzing with a simmering anger. Word had been circulating that flashy LA attorney Lucius Cockrell was in town to represent Juanita Gaddis.

Ted Logan approached his car in the Blue Bull parking lot and noticed the throng of people gathering up the street at the courthouse. He walked in that direction and noticed the stores near the square seemed to be closing early. He passed the *Boots and Hoops* shop just as a man locked the door and joined a small group heading toward the gathering. Ted followed the foursome and stood close behind them at the edge of the crowd.

"You know, we've been hearin' all day that Juanita was gonna sue Buck and J.P." The short woman pushed her carrot-colored hair away from her face with a freckled hand.

"Yeah, we've heard that too – that ungrateful little hussy! Lanny knows for a fact J.P. personally got her that job in the clerk's office."

The man standing with her was wearing a fireman's uniform. "Yeah, and J.P., Buck, *all* the deputies, *all* the firemen, we all chipped in and helped pay their medical deductible when their boy had his kidney transplant last year."

The short woman wiped her forehead with a lace handkerchief. "I do hate her husband died. I liked Willie. But they's three other women without husbands today. We've all lost a lot and we all need to stick together!"

"That's right. Juanita's got no business bringin' this big shot loudmouth down here to make up trouble when there's not none. Willie dying ain't nobody's fault but that damn Baines!"

Lucius Cockrell, wearing a bright blue silk suit and a beehive afro, strode to the microphones and pompously proclaimed, "We have seen a grave injustice here in this town! We have seen a great man, a brave public servant, die at the hands of bigotry! The Summer County sheriff's department nurtured this vicious prejudice until a bullet was fired into the heart of a black man! The sheriff is responsible! The county is –

A roar of boos and shouts erupted from the crowd. Many in the front of the group pushed forward toward the bottom steps, waving their arms and shaking fists. Ted saw there was a notable absence of any police security near the front of the courthouse. Two state troopers walked rapidly toward the steps from around the back corner as the crowd got louder.

Cockrell seemed stunned by the response and shouted above the growing din. "On behalf of the Gaddis family, I will be bringing a twenty million dollar wrongful death suit against Deputy Yancey and the Summer County sheriff's department!" As the irate assembly surged closer to the steps, the flamboyant lawyer beat a hasty retreat into the courthouse.

SEVEN

Ted got out of his car and looked around. The place had a romantic '60s appeal in its own rustic way. The marina's main building was a long rambling structure with weathered, unpainted siding and a patched tin roof. Rusty Coca-Cola and Buffalo Rock signs seemed to be holding a portion of the front wall together. Ted noticed an assortment of boats docked around an "E" shaped pier that connected directly to the back of the building. A dozen or so pickup trucks and two other cars were scattered in no particular order across the red crusty parking lot. At the sound of grinding gravel, Ted turned to see a green SUV topped with blue police lights pull up next to his rented Taurus.

The clean-cut young officer walked briskly around the front of his vehicle and said, "You must be Ted Logan. I'm Rocky Barnett." His handshake was firm but short.

"It's nice to meet you, Rocky. I appreciate your taking the time to see me."

Rocky pointed at three concrete picnic tables in a small grove of water oak trees near the shoreline. "Let's go sit down at a table." The game warden took a seat facing the lake and Logan slid his lanky frame onto the hard bench facing Rocky. "Actually Ted, we've already met once before."

"No kidding! Where was that?"

"It was in Chicago. I was a Newslink super prep, class of '80. You were at our awards dinner and wrote the story for the magazine."

Ted studied the tanned face and grinned. "Yeah, yeah. I didn't put it together when Skeeter was giving me your career highlights – but yeah, I remember you now. Number five. Paul Hornung's clone. You wore his number. You looked just like him and you ran just like him. The last great white tailback."

Rocky smiled shyly. "Well, that's what you wrote about me. Hornung was before my time so I'll have to take your word for it."

"Damn! Time flies. I haven't covered the super preps in over fifteen years. You mind if I smoke?"

"Nah. Help yourself."

Ted exhaled a cloud of smoke. "I'm sure Skeeter told you I'm here to do a story on the dog attacks. Will you help me?"

Rocky looked at Ted's craggy face, then stared out at the water. "That depends on what kind of story you're doing."

Ted tapped his cigarette ash off the table edge. "I only do one kind. I want the blunt truth with all the warts. No bullshit. I'm not politically correct and I don't give a damn whose toes I step on."

Rocky looked back into Ted's face. "You mean that, don't you?"

"Yes, I do."

Rocky bowed his head and rubbed his short sandy hair with his left hand. Neither man spoke for a long minute. "Okay, Ted. I'll help you. But I've got several problems and we have to do this my way or not at all."

"I'm listening, Rocky."

"Okay ... I don't want anybody to know I'm talking to you or any other reporter. At least for a while. I don't want anybody – most of all J.P. – to think I'm undercutting the sheriff's department. I wouldn't do that ... but there's something going on here that's just not adding up. If I can figure it out, maybe you can tell the real story."

"That's exactly what I intend to do. I'm going to camp right here in Summer until *I* understand the real story. What do you need me to do?"

"Well for starters, don't try to talk to me in town and never when I'm working for the sheriff. That's just Wednesdays and Thursdays. I'm pretty much my own boss in this county on my game and fish days, which is just about twenty-four hours a day the other five days. We can talk out here. Most of the old boys hanging around never see anybody from town anyway." He pointed to his right across a narrow inlet of water. "I live just across the slough in that log house. You're welcome there anytime – and if you really wanna stay out of sight, old Bug Pepper that owns this place, has a couple of cabins he rents out by the week. They're nothing fancy but they're cheap and nobody pays you any attention."

"That sounds like a good suggestion. I'll check into it."

Rocky turned his stare back out across the still lake. "If you want to, you can ride with me some on my game warden days. It's mostly on back roads. A lot of times at night. I can't guarantee you won't have to be put out on the side of the road sometime but …" A big smile creased his tanned face. "You don't strike me as the kinda guy that's afraid of being alone in the dark."

Ted grinned. "Well, you're right. I'm not afraid of the dark but I will be worried about some little southern belle trying to take advantage of me. So be careful *where* you drop me off."

Rocky chuckled. "Yeah, I'll try to be careful about that."

Ted lit another cigarette. "Okay. So when I'm not riding shotgun with you or lounging around here at the Summer Riviera, what do you suggest I do to get my story? Who do I need to talk to?"

"If you wanna see for yourself how this county feels about their deputies, come to Hank and Lem's funeral tomorrow. It's gonna be a double funeral at First Baptist in town. Full police honors."

"Yeah, okay. I'll do that."

"Look, you need to get there early. It starts at two. Be there before noon and, if you want my advice, don't hang out with all the other reporters. Don't bring a camera or a notebook or wear a press badge. Just show up early and try to fit in." He looked at Logan's faded Bears tee shirt. "You got one big advantage. You don't look or act like a big city reporter. You'll mix in just fine with all the local folks."

Ted nodded. "Well, I'll try to do just that."

Rocky rubbed his head again. "If you want to get a totally different take, go to Willie's funeral out in Westville on Sunday. Anybody with a white face will kinda stick out there, but I've got a friend, Jarvis Whitfield, who'll be welcomed with open arms out there. He's a retired professor who lives just up the river from me. All the black leaders

53

like him. He's always been sort of a local crusader for civil rights. If Jarvis will let you tag along, they'll treat you like royalty. And you'd better pack a lunch, they'll be funeralizing all day long. I won't be there. The Gaddis' have made it clear that nobody from the sheriff's department is welcome. And, because of that, the Alabama Peace Officers' Association is not sending a single delegate. Nobody in a uniform is likely to show up. You won't see two funerals more different."

"I'd like to attend. What about these accusations? Did Yancey really threaten to kill Gaddis?"

"I guess that depends on how you see it. Sure, Buck *said* he was going to blow Willie's brains out. He said it more'n once. Once in a bar full of people. But Buck's always popped off a lot of bull. He can be hotheaded, especially when he's had a few beers. But that was a long time ago. Buck's a good solid deputy on duty and he and Willie have been getting along fine for years. That's why J.P. could partner them up sometimes. Look, I think Juanita is all wrong to stir this back up. I don't know how Willie got shot but I'm not believing Buck did it on purpose. Willie's shot his mouth off at Buck just as much over the years."

"What do you mean?"

"Well, it goes all the way back to high school ball. Buck was a pretty big star at Summer in the 70s. Especially in basketball. Westville had an all black 1A school until 1979 and Willie was an All-State forward on their team. He and Buck are the same age, so for three or four years they played each other twice a year. The Summer-Westville basketball games used to really be a major rivalry around here. The little black school against the big 6A white school just eighteen miles apart. Well, Buck and Willie always tied up in these games. They both threw elbows and punches. They both got ejected a few times. They both spent the next ten years or so yaa-yaaing at each other. When J.P. hired Willie, Buck guaranteed he'd run him off in six weeks. Willie always gave it right back to him though."

"So did Gaddis ever threaten to kill *Yancey*?"

"Only if 'I'll cut the mother's guts out and watch him flop' is considered a death threat."

"I see. So it was mutual true love."

"Yeah, but this is mostly old stuff. They both had mellowed out a lot. They rode a lot of shifts together this last year. Heck, they're both over forty-five now and have sons that played ball together at Summer High School. Those two boys are real close friends. It's just a shame Juanita is trying to make this a race thing. It's gonna pull Summer County apart. Look Ted, I've got to run. If you get a cabin from Bug, I'll check in on you later tonight."

"Yeah, I think I'll do that."

"Okay. Bug's got a little bar and grill inside offering greasy spoon dining at its finest. Oh and by the way, if you wanna talk to Skeeter anymore, do it at the same time as yesterday. Mid-afternoon when the Bull is empty. Otherwise, folks will connect you to me pretty fast."

"Sure, that's fine with me. Skeeter Yates *is* a very interesting woman."

Rocky smiled. "Yeah, she is definitely *interesting* all right. I probably should've married her the day I graduated high school." He pushed up from the table and turned toward the parking lot. "But then Skeeter never seems to have any problem landing a husband."

Three hours later, Ted felt right at home hunkered over a Jack and water inside the smoky confines of Bug Pepper's Sportsman's Bar and Grill. Dusty deer heads and mounted bass looked down onto the ten-stool bar from every direction. Most of the time, the smell of stale cigarette smoke prevailed over the pervasive aroma of fresh fish. To Ted's amazement and delight, the joint actually had satellite TV. He sat with his whiskey and watched the special CNN report on the screen behind the bar. "Piney Bald Standoff-Day 4" was the bold caption under the picture. "Today a federal grand jury was convened to consider weapons charges against entrenched fugitive Malachi Baines. Baines and an undetermined number of family members continue to hold local and federal authorities at bay from their heavily fortified and armed encampment high in the Cane Ridge mountains of north central Alabama. Baines is wanted for questioning in a child molestation case and is believed to be the owner of large guard dogs that attacked and killed four deputies during a raid Tuesday on the remote compound. Today's grand jury inquiry is prompted by allegations of illegal weapons possession brought by the ATF. Sources within the ATF and the U.S. Marshal's office are reporting that a special FBI hostage negotiation team will first attempt to convince Baines to voluntarily surrender before agents pursue a more aggressive approach. Local Summer County officials are skeptical of the negotiation strategy and point out that due to rugged geography and natural barricades, no officer is able to get within a two-mile radius of the Baines home. Even a helicopter approach is considered risky in the often fog-shrouded mountain peaks."

Out of the corner of his eye, Ted saw the game warden walk into the dingy bar. He took a seat beside Logan and sighed heavily. Ted noticed Rocky's uniform was drenched with sweat. He pointed with his drink toward the TV screen. "The feds are trying to get a weapons warrant. It sounds like they believe once Baines is in custody, the murder and child molestation charges will follow."

Rocky propped his wet forehead on both hands and stared at the countertop. "Yeah," he said softly. "I know. I think you're exactly right."

Ted twisted on his stool. "You don't believe Baines had anything to do with the dogs or the molestation, do you?"

Rocky raised his head up and looked at Ted. "Nope. I *know* Malachi doesn't own the dogs and never touched his daughter."

Ted took a swig from his drink. "Is your opinion based on more than gut instincts?"

"Yeah … it's based on looking Malachi Baines in the eye and hearing it from his own mouth – just about two hours ago."

EIGHT

First Baptist Church   *Summer, Alabama*   *May 23, 1998*

The semi-cool air inside the packed church was heavy with the scent of antiperspirants and cologne. The stocky blonde woman beside Ted shifted her bottom and squeezed him even tighter into the corner of the back row church pew. She "whispered" again in a raspy voice you could hear from a block away. "None of this woulda happened if those mountain people weren't just animals! Yah know them men always make babies with their cousins, nieces... even their daughters! They're just vermin. Now they've made Verna and Sally widows." An older couple seated in front of her turned their heads and nodded solemnly in agreement.

Every available seat in the spacious sanctuary had been filled for over an hour, including all the folding chairs lining the outside aisles. People were now standing with their backs pressed against the arching stained glass windows. Ted could hear sobbing all around him. He was struck by the feeling of genuine sadness so pervasive in the overflow crowd.

At 1:45, a large choir in purple robes filed into position behind the pulpit and both a piano and organ began to play. The choir sang several touching songs. Ted thought it was traditional southern gospel. At two o'clock, they began a particularly moving hymn.

"Rock of Ages, cleft for me. Let me hide myself in thee…." As the slow stirring melody resonated through the stately church, a double column of police officers slowly processed from the rear of the building. In dress uniforms, they marched in deliberate, halting cadence down the middle aisle. J.P. and Spud Jordan were the lead pair. Ted recognized Rocky in the third set. He looked awkward in the formal brown coat and short brimmed hat. State troopers, county sheriffs and an assortment of officers from cities around the southeast followed the Summer deputies toward the two flag-draped coffins. As each pair reached the caskets, they paused and saluted, then marched on by to the left. The choir continued, *"While I draw this fleeting breath, when my eyes shall close in death…"* The emotion in the church was the most charged Ted Logan had ever felt.

The Fincher and Hawkins families followed the last two officers toward the front. Sally Fincher and Verna Hawkins both appeared solemn and dignified, hatless in long black dresses. The slain officers' children quietly held their mothers' hands as they moved toward the reserved front row pews. Thirty or so extended family members came behind, several of the women wiping their eyes with handkerchiefs.

Once the families were seated, two preachers took charge of the service. The older minister read some scripture before the younger one prayed a lengthy prayer. Then the senior pastor said, "Our faithful deacons gave their lives serving our community. We celebrate their wonderful examples and rejoice in their eternal reward. Timothy Hawkins and J.P. Jordan will lead us in remembering our noble brothers in Christ, Lem Hawkins and Hank Fincher."

A low collective murmur rippled through the crowd as eleven-year-old Tim Hawkins, clutching a wrinkled sheet of paper, walked resolutely up to the podium. He stood behind a short microphone and spoke without looking at his paper. "My daddy was a brave man. He always tried to help people. No matter if it was dangerous he went anyway." The slim boy sounded and looked like a little man. As he continued in his high-pitched voice, the sounds of people crying filled the church. "My daddy said sometimes he had to drive fast and go out in the dark to keep other people safe. My granddaddy was a brave man too. He died in the war before I was born. He saved a lot of marines and got a medal from the president. Grandma says I come from good stock. Someday I wanna be a marine and a deputy so I can help people like my daddy did."

Ted was drawn to the boy's simple words. He *knew* who he was. He was connected to his father and his grandfather in a way that would impact his whole life. *What would it be like to have such pride in your parents and grandparents? To even know your parents. A big city orphans' home brat was never connected to anybody or anything. It was different here in this old backwater town. Everyone was connected. They were all part of each other.*

The boy's small voice began to break. "My daddy liked to take me fishing. I'm gonna miss him now." Tears ran down his dimpled cheeks. He was a child again. Both ministers rose and embraced him. He wiped his freckled face with his notepaper as they led him back to his seat.

J.P. Jordan then slowly walked to the pulpit and faced the emotional crowd. His face held a tortured expression. He began to speak in a shaky voice. "Tim and Debbie Hawkins do come from good stock. So do Jimmy and Bobby Fincher. Their fathers were two of the finest men I ever knew. I was in the waiting room the day Lem Hawkins was born. He grew up a model kid and became a model leader in our church and in our town. Timmy's right. Lem did go out in the dark to keep other people safe. The night the old theater burned, Lem was first on the scene. He got over fifty people out by himself. Three times he went back into the smoke. The last time he got third degree burns on both arms. Scars he's carrying to his grave. Some of you in this church today are alive because Lem Hawkins was on duty that cold night in '89."

A woman two rows in front of Ted burst into uncontrolled sobs as the sheriff continued. "I've known Hank just as long. Coached him in little league. I pinned on his Eagle Scout badge and stood beside him when he married Sally. Hank was the best officer in a medical emergency we ever had. Two years ago he revived a three-year-old that almost drowned in a bathtub. Later that same shift, he worked a wreck near Maple Cove and stopped a man from bleeding to death. Hank worked as many accidents while off duty as on. There's no way to know how many lives he saved in his eighteen years with the department."

J.P. paused and looked around the church. "These two men gave us all many years of selfless service. Lem and Hank gave me their trust ...so did Willie and Charlie." The big man's voice faltered and tears came to his eyes. "They lost their lives trying to do what I asked 'em." He rubbed his eyes. "My heart is so heavy. I'd do anything on earth to change this week. It's not right. The good should be rewarded and the evil should be banished. Lem and Hank shouldn't be under those flags. They should be home with their families. I'd take their place if I could." He swallowed hard. Tears were dripping off his broad chin. "God in heaven, give the good men peace."

The woman sitting beside Ted sobbed. "Oh poor J.P. Dear man." The older minister put his arm over the sheriff's shoulder and gently ushered him down from the podium.

Both preachers then gave short sermons and the younger one led another prayer. When the prayer ended, a troop of uniformed police bagpipers assembled around the caskets. They formed a double column as a soulful tune flowed from their instruments.

Like everyone in the building, Ted was moved by the heartrending sounds. The music seemed familiar, but he couldn't quite place the song. He could hear the choir now ..."*that saved a wretch like me. I once was lost but now am found; was blind, but now I see.*"

The musicians slowly marched toward the back of the church. Six Summer County deputies picked up the first casket and proceeded behind. A mixture of police officers lifted the second coffin and followed out the wide middle aisle. The choir continued singing…"*Twas grace that taught my heart to fear, and grace my fears relieved.*"

The widows and their families followed the caskets out of the church. From his last pew vantage point, Ted could see the front steps through a back window. The steps and the sidewalk were lined with dozens of police officers. When the pallbearers reached the top step, the line of officers all snapped to attention and held a salute. Ted leaned to his left and looked up the street. There was a row of police cars with lights flashing stretching as far as he could see. News sources later reported over two hundred police cars from one hundred agencies formed an escort to the cemetery.

The policemen outside in their ceremonial uniforms remained frozen like statues as Sally Fincher and Verna Hawkins stoically led their children down the steps. On the sidewalk, the bagpipers played on. The honor guards carefully loaded the flag-draped caskets into the waiting hearses as the haunting song continued. *"When we've been there ten thousand years, bright shining as the sun. We've no less days to sing God's praise, than when we first begun."*

NINE

A technician wearing a headset looked at the nervous reporter and gave him a thumbs up "go" signal. The young Fox correspondent put on his serious stage face. "I am standing just outside the police command center in the remote mountain community of Tate's Gap, Alabama. This is day five of the standoff with armed cult members and a day when Summer County buried two of their slain officers." The television cameras panned to the beehive of activity in an open grassy field. "Behind me you can see a staging area that has the look of an army preparing for a major invasion. Those gray tank-like vehicles you are seeing belong to the FBI's special operations unit. The FBI, ATF, U.S. Marshals and Alabama National Guard all have specialized units and equipment in place to supplement state and local police officers. As you can see, most of the officers on the scene have a military appearance with their camouflaged fatigues, combat helmets and automatic weapons. I can see at least ten armored vehicles being prepared including several army tanks assigned to the National Guard. I am told it may prove to be nearly impossible to deploy any of this heavy armament. Malachi Baines and his supporters are holed up high on a small mountaintop plateau known as Piney Bald. On the north and west, Piney Bald is protected by sheer rock cliffs that plunge over four hundred feet into thick forest. To approach from the east requires crossing a formidable swamp at the base of the mountain. This vast wetland, known as Junee Bottoms, is where attack dogs killed four Summer County deputies last Tuesday. The only road up the mountain is a narrow, winding eight-mile passage that runs north from here in Tate's Gap. Approximately two miles from the Baines' encampment, the road crosses a deep gorge high above Coon Creek. A shaky wooden bridge is all that spans the ravine. Authorities here are not certain the heavy assault vehicles can safely cross the small bridge. This is complicated by the fact that approaching on foot places officers in danger of snipers and the killer dogs. So they prepare and wait. There are enough men, firepower and equipment now in Tate's Gap to conquer a small country. However, the rugged Alabama mountains and a few large dogs may render all this high-tech law enforcement muscle virtually useless."

Dye's Landing, Summer County   *7:00 pm*   *May 23, 1998*

Ted sat alone at the end of the bar and poured catsup over his plate of hash browns. The poignant images from his day were still fresh in his mind. Flags at half mast all over town. Hundreds of people lining the route to the cemetery and crying as the funeral procession passed. He took a bite of his food and noticed Bug Pepper staring at him from behind the bar. Bug walked closer and propped both elbows on the bar. Pepper resembled a polar bear with a red nose. His shock of white hair, bushy eyebrows and thick grizzled beard covered most of his face. "Everybody's pretty upset 'round here. All those folks in town want Malachi's hide."

65

Ted looked at the bar owner. "Yeah. It seems to me the locals are definitely forming a lynch mob. I assume you don't believe Baines is responsible for the deaths."

"Sha! Malachi ain't responsible fer none of them things."

"Why do you say that?"

"I know 'im. He's almost kinfolk. My mama was a Tate. Malachi's wife's my third cousin. Shoot, me an' Malachi used to coon hunt. I run with him fer twenty years. Ain't no way he'd hurt his girl, an' he ain't never had no dogs that would bite that way. Old Malachi'd git shed of a bluetick if'n it was too ill at a tree. Shoot, even his hog dogs is gentle. You'n just walk right up an' pet 'em."

"Bug, why do all the people in town seem convinced Malachi Baines is guilty?"

Pepper took a bottle of Wild Turkey from the shelf behind him and poured a straight shot into a coffee cup. "Them people in town thinks they's better than mountain folks. I've heard 'em say all the hill families is just trash. It ain't hard to git 'em stirred up 'bout hanging a mountain man. They believes we's all jist savages." He downed the shot of whiskey and wiped his mouth on a soiled t-shirt sleeve. "They don't know much 'bout huntin' dogs or the woods neither. If'n they did, they'd know nobody coulda sicced them kinda dogs on the deputies. They's just wild dogs."

Bug went back to the grill and Ted progressed from fried potatoes to cold whiskey. A voice from the TV set behind the bar grabbed his attention. He leaned closer as the newsman said, "Let me warn you, the picture you are about to see will be very disturbing to some viewers. It graphically displays the outcome of a brutal blood sport. CNN today obtained this exclusive photo of cultist fugitive Malachi Baines and his two sons. The picture was taken in Summer, Alabama less than one year ago." The screen displayed a photograph of Malachi, Zack and Jesse Baines straddling two huge dead hogs. Posed on either side of the three was a dog with a large head. Bright red blood was evident on both dogs, the hogs and the hunters. Jesse Baines' smiling face was painted with blood. "The large dogs in the photo belong to the Baines family," the announcer continued. "Sources close to the investigation tell CNN these dogs are virtually identical to the guard dogs killed by officers during the raid last week. The dogs in the photo are used to locate and attack wild pigs. Dog behavior experts tell us dogs with this aggressive disposition could easily be trained to attack humans. Investigators say the photo is a tangible piece of evidence linking Baines to the murders of four deputies."

Piney Bald, Summer County   *12:00 midnight*   *May 24, 1998*

The rusty iron wash-pot boiled and bubbled. The hickory coals under the pot glowed bright orange as a thick putrid smoke escaped through the cracks in the small shack's ceiling. Granny Tate poked the coals with a green sapling stick then limped over to a table on the back wall of her medicine shed. She picked up a tin cup and hobbled back to pour its contents into her boiling brew. "Hawk's eye and a cat's heart,'" she murmured as she dumped in the smelly contents and slung the cup's slimy residue onto the dirt floor. She took a long piece of bone from her apron pocket and waved it over the pot. "Sun an' moon, wind an' rain. Cast out the demons et curse my Callie. Burn tha devil man in tha fires of hell!"

TEN

Hundreds of black faces and white paper fans were inside the modest church. Ted had never been in a large, all-black gathering before. He felt obvious and uncomfortable. He and his host, Jarvis Whitfield, attempted to slide unobtrusively into a back row pew. The two white men had just sat down when a committee of ushers greeted them and insisted they move to the front "deacons' pew."

They were then escorted down the main aisle to the open casket where the ushers paused to allow them to view the body. Ted was surprised to see Willie Gaddis laid out in a shiny green suit and red tie. He had assumed the body would be clothed in the deputy's uniform.

The deacons' pew was a single church bench positioned perpendicular to the regular pews and just a few feet from the pulpit. It appeared to be the seat of honor. Ted assumed Jarvis Whitfield's status within the black community accounted for their special treatment. There was one other white person in the church – an older lady seated beside them. *Maybe just being white made you a VIP at this funeral.*

Ted glanced at the program he had been handed at the door. A color photo of Willie taken at least twenty years ago covered the front page. Ted looked around the crowded sanctuary. The building felt air-conditioned but practically all the women were waving paper fans. Just to his right, six women stood in a row with their backs to the wall. They each wore a yellow ribbon stamped with the word "USHER" pinned to their dress. The closest woman in the row momentarily stopped fanning and Ted read the writing on her wooden-handled fan. One side was an advertisement for Jackson Brothers Funeral Home. When she moved the fan again, he saw the opposite side was a picture of Jesus surrounded by sheep.

The church was full except for the two left front pews that were apparently reserved for the family. Most of the women in the crowd wore fancy hats, some quite elaborate. The men sported a wide variety of styles and colors of dress suits. The sedate manner of the assembly struck Ted. No one in the church was actually crying. They sat and fanned and waited as if for a concert.

Twenty minutes after the funeral was scheduled to begin, there was a stirring in the crowd and murmurs near the back. Ted could hear someone wailing. At about that same time, a man in a powder blue tuxedo began playing a console organ. A short preacher, holding a raised Bible in front of his face, began a slow march down the short center aisle. He was reading scripture at the top of his lungs. Juanita Gaddis stepped inside the church and let out a harrowing scream. Ted almost jumped out of his seat. Juanita continued screaming and swung her arms wildly like a crazed woman. Three male ushers surrounded and attempted to subdue her. They finally contained her flailing arms, but when they tried to move her forward down the aisle, she locked her legs and fought them like a tiger, crying "No! No! No!" The preacher kept moving and reading louder and louder. By the time he reached the altar, he was shouting to be heard above

Juanita's shrieking. The ushers half pulled and half carried the kicking widow down the aisle as her family followed behind. There was too much yelling to even hear the organ.

Juanita was released just in front of the casket. She screeched again, "No! Oh, no!" and dove head first over the body, knocking floral arrangements askew. The coffin on a rolling dolly slammed back against the altar rail. The ushers rushed forward to retrieve her but she was gripping the backside of the casket with both hands and kicking her legs in the air. "Oh, baby! Oh, baby!" She shouted with her face pressed down on top of the corpse.

Ted was in shock. He had never witnessed such extraordinary behavior. The ushers eventually extracted Juanita from Willie's body and all but body-slammed her into her reserved seat. Willie's mother and sister repeated Juanita's screaming dive for the body as they took their turn at the coffin. After being pried loose, the mother fainted. When she was revived, she resumed her fight with the ushers. It took a dozen ushers nearly thirty minutes to get the three women anchored in their pews. Once seated, they still had to be restrained. While the male ushers held them down, the six female ushers standing against the wall moved into action. They formed a line in front of the family and fanned them continuously with their paper fans. *"The designated fanners"*. Juanita and her mother-in-law would continue to mumble and groan for the next two hours.

The casket was closed for the final time as about two dozen women in matching dark dresses assembled behind the pulpit. You could hear the organ now and the choir joined in a rhythmic song. As they sang, the chorus line swayed back and forth in unison. As the singers swayed, the subdued audience became vocal. Many clapped their hands in time to the music and shouts of "Yes!" and "Yes, Jesus!" erupted around the room.

Ted recognized the soulful sound. It reminded him of the music played in a Chicago blues club. He had heard it called "cotton field gospel." When the song ended, a bulky preacher with snow-white hair read a long passage of scripture, after which yet another preacher led the people in prayer. Over the next hour, five different pastors either prayed, preached or read from the Bible. About every fifteen minutes, the women's choir would render another singing and swaying number.

Ted could not take his eyes off Willie's family. It was hard to tell if the Gaddis women were displaying profound grief or merely performing their expected roles in the community drama. He stared at Willie's teenaged son. He, like most male family members, wore a tuxedo. The boy seemed to be genuinely mourning his father, periodically wiping his eyes with the sleeve of his tux.

In the middle of the third minister's sermon, Juanita Gaddis suddenly sprang to her feet, bolted up the aisle and out the back door, wailing with every step. The preacher continued speaking as if nothing had happened. Five minutes later, a group of ushers again dragged Juanita, kicking and screaming, back to the pew. The preacher calmly continued as if her hysteria were an every day event.

The "sermonizing" climaxed when the church's senior minister took his turn. The lanky man, wearing a black and gold clerical robe, shouted out a few lines in a singsong cadence. The organist immediately responded with a few corresponding high notes from the electronic keyboard. The preacher would chant, the organ would follow in rhythm with a short burst, the crowd would shout "Tell it, brother!" or "Amen, brother!" The high-energy mix of chanting a sermon to music and audience participation fascinated Ted.

Two hours into the service, the eulogies started and an already strange funeral got even stranger. The senior pastor announced the first eulogizer, Lucius Cockrell. Ted was stunned. The LA lawyer stepped up to the podium and immediately launched into a racially charged diatribe. In his own chanting delivery he railed, "This good man died at the hands of a white man's bullet! We've been shackled and beaten and shot by cruel overseers for two hundred yeahs....Our brother Willie Gaddis is just de latest victim! He refused to go to de back of de bus and paid de ultimate price!" Cockrell didn't get electric organ music after each line, but he did get rounds of amens!

Ted was uncomfortable again. It felt like the verbose attorney was blaming the three white people in the church for the sins of slavery and somehow this blame extended to Willie's death. *Didn't the arrogant son-of-a-bitch know the slaves had been free in Summer County for one hundred thirty-four years! All the "ameners" apparently didn't get the news either. It was offensive. This was no eulogy. This was no longer a funeral. It was a shameless attempt by a rank outsider to stir the flames of racial hatred for his own mercenary aims.* Cockrell went on to blame the Summer County sheriff's department for every misfortune the black race had endured before he finally shut up and sat down.

After the twenty minutes of charged demagoguery, the emotional pace of the funeral slowed. Two people gave short traditional homage to the deceased, then floral and grief card tributes began. For over thirty minutes, the funeral home staff held up cards received by the Gaddis family and called the names of the senders. Then there was a call for all Willie's nieces and nephews to assist in removing the flowers from the church. About a dozen young black men and women came forward and picked up floral arrangements, one at a time. Before each arrangement was carted out of the church, the funeral home staff acknowledged the person who sent it. It took another forty minutes to move out all the flowers.

Finally, the senior pastor led a closing prayer. The choir swayed and sang one more time to the organ music and the ushers escorted the still screaming Gaddis women down the aisle.

Ted and Jarvis got outside just in time to see the family being driven away in five stretch limousines. It was a very short ride as the limos transported the family about two hundred feet to Willie's gravesite just behind the small brick church.

When Ted climbed back into Jarvis Whitfield's '62 Studebaker, it was after six o'clock. They had been inside the church for over five hours. Ted was totally exhausted, in nicotine withdrawals and in need of a men's room, fast. Jarvis and his old relic car didn't seem to hurry anywhere.

As they poked along down a country back road, Jarvis nonchalantly took a videocassette out of his coat pocket and flipped it onto Ted's lap. "Lucius Cockrell was handing these out, so I got an extra for you. He says this proves Yancey was planning to kill Willie just two days before the shooting."

Ted reclined with a beer in the rough-hewn comfort of Rocky's cabin. Rocky was as anxious as Ted to view the video Jarvis had gotten from Cockrell. He pushed the cassette into his VCR and sat down with the remote control. "I've been hearing about this all day long. They say it's x-rated. Tonya's supposed to be drunk as a skunk and naked!"

Ted sipped his beer. "Tonya is Buck Yancey's wife?"

"Yeah. Buck's wife and everybody's favorite ex-stripper."

"Stripper! I thought all the women down here just baked pies and went to prayer meetings."

Rocky chuckled. "Well, let's just say Tonya's not the kinda girl most men would take home to momma. Buck and all the other guys in town think she's a real prize. Most of the women won't speak to her. She's Buck's second wife. I guess his answer to mid-life crisis."

"What do you think about her?"

Rocky popped the top off a Bud Lite. "I wouldn't take her home to momma, either, but I'd sure stuff a dollar in her garter belt! You're fixin' to see for yourself."

He pushed the play button. The picture was fuzzy, obviously an amateur home video. White print at the bottom right read *5-16-98 8:47 pm.* A party scene played out on the screen with men and women in their thirties and forties filling beer mugs from a hose attached to a silver keg. The group was all white. Rocky froze the frame. "The big guy in the Braves t-shirt – that's Buck." The scene rolled forward. The gang was getting

74

louder and sillier. Rocky stopped the tape again. "And *that* is Tonya!" The twisting blonde in the center of the picture was wearing a halter-top fashioned from the confederate battle flag with skin-tight short shorts. When Rocky resumed the video, the men started shouting, "Show us your tits! Show us your tits!" Tonya and a tall redhead were in a contest to be the first to comply. They both raised their shirts and flashed large breasts for the camera. Then Tonya ripped off the flag blouse and twirled it over her head. "Man, that's a fine set," Rocky groaned.

Ted nodded. "There *are* some nice melon patches down here." As they continued watching, Buck lifted Tonya and set her on his shoulder. She squealed and waved her halter flag. Buck shouted, "Salute the Stars and Bars boys! The South's gonna rise again!"

A man with a long ponytail ran into the scene with a beer mug in each hand. He handed one mug to Buck as he kept his eyes glued to Tonya's bouncing breasts. "Right on, Bucko! When the south rises, we're gonna put those damn blacks back in their place!"

"Damn straight we will Catfish!"

Tonya held Buck's neck with one hand and nimbly used her other hand to wiggle out of her tight white shorts. Buck chugged the mug of beer. Now, completely nude, she shifted from Buck's broad left shoulder and wrapped her legs around his neck.

Rocky glanced at Ted. "Oh, man. We're gonna have to run this several times."

Tonya was now twirling her shirt high above her head with one hand. Ponytail man handed her a mug and gave her butt a quick rub. Then he yelled in Buck's ear, "Bucko, they ain't gonna make that uppity Gaddis a sergeant afore you, are they?"

Buck spun Tonya around and glared at the man. "Hell no Fish! I'm gonna blow his black ass away the first chance I get!"

The screen went to static and Rocky hit the rewind button. Ted sat his beer can down. "Who do you suppose gave Cockrell the video?"

"That's a good question. I recognized most of these people and they're not what you'd call civil rights sympathizers…but probably a hundred dollar bill and a case of Coors coulda bought it."

ELEVEN

Ted hesitated inside the door and looked around the Blue Bull dining room. The place was deserted again. Skeeter saw him coming and set a hot cup of coffee in front of him as he took a seat at the bar. "Coffee black," she said, "and no menu."

He grinned. "So you remember."

"Oh, yeah. We don't get many big tipper *celebrities* in here."

"Thank you, but I'm not sure I qualify in either category." He sipped his coffee. "I guess celebrity is in the eye of the beholder."

She propped her chin on both hands and stared at him from just a few feet away. He could smell her shampoo. *Geez, she was pretty.* "You been spending a lotta time with Rocky I hear."

"Yes, I have. I guess I'm checked in at the Dye's Landing Hilton for the duration."

"Whatta you think 'bout it out there?"

He couldn't take his eyes off her. "It's not Palm Springs but I suppose it has its own charm. What do you think about it?"

"Oh, I don't know. I don't really like going out there, I guess. Rocky's place. Bug's ole diner. It's all just a man's kinda world." She stepped back from the bar and put her hands on her small waist. "When a woman's out there, she feels like she's just there to work by the hour!"

Ted laughed and she flashed that heart-winning smile of hers. "Look, it's none of my business, but reporters are trained to ask the tough questions. Why hasn't Rocky Barnett married you?"

She blushed and fiddled with the ball of shiny hair on top of her head. "Oh, I don't know. Maybe you should ask Rocky. He thinks I'm damaged goods, I guess."

"What does that mean?"

Skeeter crossed her arms and frowned. "You're gettin' awful personal for somebody I don't know. I guess I'll tell you though since you don't know nobody 'round here anyway…Rocky didn't want me to marry Jake Plummer or Billy Cox. Now I'm a two-time divorcee with a reputation."

"Hell, it's his own fault. Why didn't he marry you himself years ago?"

She shrugged her shoulders. "Rocky just likes his space. He's too busy for a full-time wife. Maybe someday. He knows where I'm at. You want more coffee?"

"Yes please."

"I'll be back in two shakes."

Ted drained his coffee cup and watched her twist back to the counter with a full pot. "Yah know what I just heard?"

"What did you just hear?"

"Chic Johnson told me that Ellis is in this sorta trance. He ain't spoke a word to nobody since he got to the hospital. Chic says his eyes is open but he acts like he don't see or hear nobody."

"Dave Ellis – the deputy that was seriously injured?"

"Yeah…He's such a sweet man. Lots of people hate him I reckon 'cause he's got a black wife and brown kids." Her dark eyes got big. "You know them dogs chewed off his…his thing! I just can't imagine how a man would feel 'bout losing his…you know."

Ted winced with real sympathy pains. "Yeah, I damn sure can't imagine that either."

The door opened and Ted could hear voices behind him. "Well Skeeter, it sounds like you have paying customers on the way. I'm out of here." He laid a ten-dollar bill on the counter. "The change is yours."

She picked up the bill and examined it as if checking for counterfeit. "You're working your way right up my ladder. Bring all those twenties next time."

Summer Regional Medical Center   Summer, Alabama   May 26, 1998

As Ted approached Buck Yancey's hospital room door, a uniformed security guard stood up from his chair and crossed his stubby arms. Ted handed the scowling man his press credentials. "I'm Ted Logan with Newslink. Buck is expecting me."

The guard shifted his gun belt under a large pot-gut and walked into the room without speaking. Ted was not sure if he was expected to follow. In a few minutes the red-faced man returned. "You can go in now. Buck says because of Rocky, he'll talk to you. We ain't lettin' no more reporters in."

Ted entered the room and stood beside the bed. Buck Yancey was a huge man. His body was too long for the hospital bed. He was propped up in an elevated position and two large hairy arms extended from the hospital gown. Both legs were heavily bandaged.

"Thanks for seeing me, Mr. Yancey."

Buck shrugged his wide shoulders. "I can't do much else but talk."

"How are your injuries?"

"I ain't got nothing but stitches from my thighs to my toes. But I reckon it could be a lot worse. I'm the lucky one in the bunch." Yancey's voice was low and soft. It didn't match his hulk of a frame.

"Do you have a clear memory of the dog attack?"

The deputy looked at Ted. "Yeah, I've relived it all 'bout a hundred times." His brown eyes were warm. This was not the kind of man Ted had expected.

"Tell me how you remember it."

The big man folded his hands and stared out the window. "Me 'n Willie was busting through the briars, trying to stay even with Lem and Ellis. I had my hunting gloves on for the stickers but Willie's hands was taking a beatin'. We heard somebody scream in the radio. I reckon it was Hank. Then a coupla shots and more screams. We tried to raise Spud on the radio but couldn't get him. We started running. It was hot. We was both sweatin' like hogs."

"Willie kept tripping and falling. I hollered at him to drop his helmet and vest. I reckon he did. I shucked my lid but the zipper was stuck on my bulletproof, so I just wore it and kept running. With Willie falling down so much, Ellis and Lem caught up pretty quick. Then we heard Spud's double zero. The next thing I know, I look behind me and a big sonofabitch dog's got Lem by the neck." Yancey swallowed hard. His eyes were moist. "Ellis yanked out his piece and tried to get a bead on the dog. He was moving toward the SOB and stepped on another one." He shook his head as his voice faltered. "It grabbed Ellis and tore him apart. I seen blood all over him." Buck wiped his eyes. "Everything just got crazy then. Ellis was yelling, but I seen him shoot the one that had him. Then I glimpsed two more coming right at us from the trees. A black one and a red one. I twisted around and opened up on them with the scattergun. I reckon I got 'em both. I busted the red one three times. I sorta remember hearing two pistols blazing away behind me. I turned around and dropped the shotgun. Willie was down right behind me and a dog with a white head was shaking Willie's arm. I pulled out my Glock and nailed that bastard dog right in the head with one shot. It just dropped right on top of Willie. I never seen Lem again the whole time. It got quiet and Ellis…Ellis was crying and holding hisself. He had his hunting gloves on too, and they was solid red with blood." Yancey started sobbing. "I…I never seen anything so pitiful. Ellis…Ellis is my huntin' partner – my best friend. I went over and tried to help stop the bleeding." He paused and blew his nose on a tissue. "Down between his legs was all just like bloody hamburger." He sniffed twice. "I was bent over Ellis when the last two grabbed my legs from behind. I never even heard 'em coming. They chewed into both legs. I tried to kick 'em loose. I never felt so much pain before. I was on my belly and couldn't get the

Glock back out of the holster. I finally pulled it loose and got a shot into one of 'em. I guess I just gut shot 'im. It started yelping and ran off. When it did, the other one chased after it, growling like crazy. I tried to get off another shot but never did. I couldn't make my legs move. I called Spud and said they was all down. I could see Willie wasn't moving so I crawled back to Ellis on my elbows and put pressure on his crotch. I didn't even know I was bleeding bad 'til Lip and the others got there."

Ted was spellbound by the poignant account. He was having difficulty reconciling this man in front of him with the one he had seen on the videotape. He cleared his throat. "You only fired two shots from your handgun?"

"Yeah, just two."

"And you definitely remember both shots?"

"Yeah. One in the white-headed dog that had Willie's arm and the last dog that had me."

Ted saw sadness in Buck's face.

"I know what you're getting at. I didn't shoot Willie."

Ted looked the deputy in the eye. "I've seen a video where you promised to blow him away."

Buck ducked his head and nodded. "Yeah, I said it, but I didn't really mean it. Me 'n Willie's been poppin' off since we was kids. If you could ask him, he'd tell you hisself. Willie had gotten to be my buddy. The day before this all happened, me 'n Willie 'n Ellis 'n Jocko was all out at the range together. We shot about a hundred rounds apiece and then all had a beer." He shook his head. "I get a little loud 'n crazy when I'm off sometimes…but I'd never hurt Willie."

Ted closed his notebook and studied Yancey's pained expression. He believed the deputy was telling the truth.

TWELVE

Ted stared out the side window into the pitch black. No street lights. No house lights. Nothing but darkness. They had not seen another set of headlights in half an hour. Riding night patrol with Rocky had so far been a voyage through the emptiness of rural Summer County.

Rocky broke the bored quiet. "You have a family in Chicago?"

"No. Not unless you call a boxer and a landlady a family."

"So, you're like me ... a confirmed bachelor?"

"It's not confirmed and I've got three ex-wives to prove it."

"Yeah, I hear that all the time. Maybe that's why I stay single. It's always cheaper than a divorce."

Ted twisted around in his seat belt. "I've tried and failed enough to know, so I'm offering you a piece of advice. If you don't marry Skeeter Yates, you're a damn fool. A woman like her only comes along once and you've already blown nearly twenty years."

Rocky didn't answer for a long minute. "If I ever did marry – Skeeter would probably be the one. My world's in this patrol car. I'm probably gonna get popped one night by a spotlighter. It wouldn't be fair to bring Skeeter or anybody else into this kinda life."

"That's a bunch of bullshit. A woman who loves you tries to make your world her own and you do the same for her. You're just too damn selfish to let her in."

"So after five days here you're an expert on what's wrong with my life?"

"Maybe not. But after fifty years I'm an expert on what's always been wrong with mine."

They rode again in a long silence. Suddenly, the radio blared and Ted jumped. "R-12. R-12. Request immediate assistance at the Coosa Track Lounge. Are you 10-8, Rocky?"

Rocky grabbed the mike. "I've got you Rita Jo. I'm ten minutes south on Indian River Road – what's the situation?"

"A fight with injuries and 10-32s."

"10-4. R-12 en route, code 3."

Rocky flipped on his lights and siren as he accelerated. "Hang on tight. I don't have time to let you out."

Ted gripped the dashboard. "What are 10-32s?"

"Men with guns." Rocky switched off the game and fish radio and turned to the county channel. "R-12 on sheriff's frequency. Who else is close Rita Jo?"

"D-23 is crossing Walston Bridge and R-10 is right behind him. You're gonna be first Rocky. Be careful."

The tires squealed around the curves of the narrow road. The radio was broadcasting comments from the other deputies and the dispatcher. Ted gathered the incident involved a racial confrontation. "What do you think is happening?"

Rocky's voice sounded calm and matter-of-fact. "We get a lot of trouble out at the Coosa Track. It's a redneck bar that's close to a black community. Sometimes black kids go in there just to cause trouble. There's always more guns in that place than Budweisers. With Juanita stirring up all this mess about Willie, I've been expecting something like this to happen."

Ted could see neon lights up ahead. Rocky skidded to a halt on the shoulder about a block away and keyed his mike. "R-12 on the scene. I'm going in." He stepped out of the vehicle and reached back to remove a shotgun locked between the front seats. "*Do not* get out of the truck and no matter what...don't touch the radio!"

"I'll stay put. Watch yourself in there."

Rocky smiled. "If you hear a couple of shotgun blasts, it's no big deal. I'll probably blow a hole in the ceiling so they'll all hit the deck." He turned and walked toward the bar as if he were merely strolling in to buy a drink.

Ted rolled down his window. He could hear a distant siren. In about thirty seconds, he heard two quick shots from inside the building. A man ran from the bar and jumped into a truck, slinging gravel as he sped away. A few minutes later, Rocky's voice came over the radio. "10-26. 10-26. Situation under control. I've got a runner going north, possibly Lute Gaines in a white pickup. We've got multiple injuries – some serious – request medical assistance."

Rita Jo answered, "10-4, R-12. EMT units en route. D-23, proceed north on Indian River Road. 10-38 white pickup traveling at high rate of speed, possible suspect Lute Gaines. R-10, assist R-12 at Coosa Track Lounge. D-9, code 3 to Coosa Track."

Ted listened intently to the transmissions. He had spent enough hours with a Chicago PD scanner to follow the action. He remembered 10-26 was the coded message that an officer was detaining suspects. Rocky must be holding one or more shooters inside the joint. A sheriff's car raced past with blue lights flashing and siren blasting. Apparently this was deputy D-23 in pursuit of the guy in the white pickup. Ted marveled at the sheriff department's strategy. They seemed comfortable leaving Rocky alone without an immediate back-up to hold fort in a room full of drunk men with guns while the closest deputy chased off after a vehicle already miles away. It was another eight minutes before the next deputy, R-10, sped up to the front of the bar and ran inside.

Ted pieced together that two white males and one black male had been struck by gunfire. One of the white males was seriously injured. Rocky and Jamey Ginn, R-10, arrested three white and two black suspects. In the process they recovered six handguns. A fourth white suspect escaped through a side door. Within fifteen minutes, Sam Gibson, D-23, had somehow located the white pickup and arrested Lute Gaines. Ted had been sitting in the parked Tahoe over thirty minutes before the first EMT unit arrived, followed closely by a second unit and three ambulances. Finally, two more deputy cars and a state trooper arrived to assist in transporting the prisoners.

Ted shook his head. This type of incident anywhere in Chicago would have commanded dozens of officers and rescue vehicles within minutes. He lit a cigarette and thought of a great irony. On the other side of the county, a battalion-sized force of agents with armored vehicles and helicopters was assembling to deal with the threat of three or four dogs, while here, a lone game warden with a twelve-gauge shotgun had just quickly quelled a shootout involving at least six gunmen.

Dye's Landing, Summer County   *May 27, 1998*

Graceful blue-tinted swallows skimmed the surface of the tranquil lake, scooping up bugs. A redheaded woodpecker hammered a majestic longleaf pine with a *rat-a-tat-tat* cadence. The view from Rocky's front porch was the most peaceful Ted Logan had ever soaked in. The intoxicating spring beauty made it difficult for him to focus on the police report in his lap.

Earlier in the day, Rocky had met Ted at Morrison's Crossroads to give him a copy of the Alabama Bureau of Investigation's report on the death of Willie Gaddis. Rocky had learned that, based on the ABI investigation, the state attorney general was set to announce Buck Yancey's murder indictment at four o'clock today. Ted finished reading the report just as Rocky's SUV rolled up the gravel driveway.

Rocky pulled the tan deputy's shirt out of his pants as he walked up the split-log front steps. "I hate this darn scratchy uniform. Especially on pain-in-the-ass days like today." He took off the shirt and slung it across the banister before plopping down in a rocking chair.

"Tough day?"

"Yeah. I spent the whole shift up at Tate's Gap with the feds. I'm tired of their bullshit."

Ted glanced at the woodpecker on the pine. "What's going on up there?"

"Well, for one thing, they've got the whole Army Corps of Engineers out there working on the old bridge over Coon Creek. They seem bound damn determined to prop it up so they can roll up the mountain with the third armored division or whatever the hell they've got. They're trucking in a million dollars worth of steel beams. Your taxpayers' dollars at work." He pulled off his heavy boots and propped his sock feet on the cedar railing. "Then they've ingeniously decided if they can get a message to Malachi, he'll just jog down the hill and shake hands with 'em. They've been trying to use a loudspeaker out of a helicopter to talk with him for two days. Then they got real smart and dropped a thousand of these leaflets on Piney Bald." He pulled a crumpled piece of orange paper from his pocket and tossed it to Ted. "This tells him if only he will bring himself down to Tate's Gap, unarmed, they will help him work out a *solution*." Rocky laughed. "Malachi's probably grateful they dropped him a year's supply of orange toilet paper."

Ted looked up from the FBI's flyer. "I take it you don't expect Baines to accept their generous offer."

"Malachi's a lot smarter than they are. He knows you don't trade somebody a dollar for a dime."

Rocky stood and walked into the house, returning with two cold beers. He handed one to Ted and opened the other. "And, on top of all this, they indict Buck for murder today. Five minutes later, that s-o-b Cockrell files a twenty-million dollar suit against J.P., Buck and the sheriff's department." Rocky looked over at Ted. "I've been here all my life and I've never seen the county like this. We're on the verge of a race war. The Thomas kid that got shot last night at Coosa Track is probably gonna die. If he does, this place is going to explode. I took down three new KKK signs this morning on Highway 70. We've never had that kinda stuff in Summer, not even in the sixties. If Buck goes to trial, I don't know what might happen."

Ted picked up the ABI report off the pine wood floor. "This report doesn't match several things Buck Yancey told me. The ABI says Yancey's handgun discharged five shots. Buck is very clear he only fired two."

"Yeah, I know he says that. Unfortunately for Buck, he also says he's positive it was loaded with fifteen rounds. It was definitely missing five at the end of the day. Maybe Buck got confused in the heat of the battle."

Ted flipped a page. "They say where all the brass was recovered paints a confused picture."

Rocky sipped his beer. "I know. I saw that myself. Buck moved toward Willie and Ellis when he did shoot his glock. Willie was twisting and turning and shooting. Ellis shot. Most all the 9mm brass fell in a three-foot circle and could have come from any direction."

"The report indicates a multi-colored ninety-five pound animal was found lying dead across Willie's legs," Ted said. "Buck told me the dog he shot had a white head and fell on top of Gaddis. Do you think the multi-colored dog and the dog with the white head are the same?"

"Yeah, I do. I loaded up all the dead dogs. Only one had any white markings at all. Three were solid black and one was a kinda reddish brown. The white-headed one had his brains hanging out. And Stanley Wilson told me later he thought the slug had lodged against this white one's skull."

"Is Wilson the local vet?"

"Yeah. He examined all the dogs first before the state took them down to Montgomery."

Ted lit a cigarette and looked at Rocky. "Then there's something missing here. Buck says *he* shot the white dog in the head. The report says this dog had Gaddis' blood on its teeth, so that matches Buck's story that the dog had Willie's arm. The only other dog killed dead on the spot was the black one that Dave Ellis apparently shot at point blank range. The ABI builds their case against Buck by matching the bullet in Willie's chest to Yancey's weapon. Why didn't they retrieve the slug from the white dog for a ballistics test? Or look for a slug in other dogs?"

Rocky tapped his empty beer can. "I don't know. But I don't see how that could help Buck. His slug *was* in Willie's body. The white-headed dog *was* standing over Willie. If they found Buck's slug in that dog, it would only prove that Buck was shooting damn close to Willie."

"Exactly! Don't you think they would have been anxious to add this supporting detail to their conclusion?"

Rocky nodded. "I'll find out. I've got a buddy. An old Auburn teammate with the ABI. I'll ask about that little item."

Ten days after the dog attack on the deputies, Summer County endured another casualty. Summer resident Josh Thomas died from gunshot wounds inflicted by Clenzo Langham three days earlier at the Coosa Track Lounge. The death of the young white man at the hands of a black shooter inflamed emotions to the boiling point. Racial confrontations were reported across the county by news outlets throughout the day.

Against this charged backdrop, Ted Logan faxed his first article from Summer County to his editor, Susan Rollins. The Monday, June 1st cover of *Newslink* featured a photo of the Summer County courthouse and Logan's feature title: *Summer Clash of Cultures*. "Alabama's oldest town is seething with a rage born of tragedy," Ted wrote. "On May 19, the historic community suffered the shockingly bizarre deaths of four well-known sheriff deputies. In the days since, a white officer with openly racist views has been charged with the death of the one black deputy among the four. A reclusive mountain man with a criminal history is widely blamed by local residents for the deaths of all four deputies. Last Friday's racially motivated shooting death of a twenty-one-year-old white man comes after a week in which Summer's black community was whipped into a frenzy by outside civil rights activists. The events of the past two weeks have elicited blatantly biased passions long simmering below the serene surface of Summer County. The aftermath of the tragic episode now pits whites against blacks and townspeople against mountain families in a county with little prior history of ethnic conflict."

The story related the details of the attorney general's case against Buck Yancey, the history of Willie and Buck's relationship and Ted's interview with the accused deputy. "The nation follows the dog attack saga with a morbid fascination as an army of federal agents prepare to storm an Appalachian family's wilderness home." Ted concluded, "The alleged murder of Willie Gaddis by his fellow deputy has become an explosive subplot to the drama of Malachi Baines' culpability for all the officers' deaths. Politics and prejudice seem destined to determine the ultimate consequences from a fateful day in the pristine mountains of north Alabama."

THIRTEEN

J.P. Jordan leaned on the rail of his back deck gripping a steaming mug of coffee with one large hand. The first pink rays of the morning sun were barely visible in the eastern sky. The sheriff's dawn solitude was broken when his wife slammed the patio door on her way to join him.

"Gosh sugar, you're out awfully early for a Saturday." She tripped over his large boots on the deck floor and caught herself on the railing. "You must have an early tee time with the boys."

J.P. looked over his shoulder at Marabell. "I've been awake since three. Can't sleep anymore. Don't even want to think about playing golf."

She put her hand on his shoulder. "Oh, sugarplum, *I know* exactly what you're going through. You've just got to stop blaming yourself for this awful, awful tragedy. It's not your fault. It's nobody's fault but that evil Baines man."

The sheriff sipped from his mug and stared at the sunrise. "Every day for thirty-six years I've made decisions that affect people's lives. I've tried to do the right thing. I'm sixty-four years old and my old man's been gone thirty years, but I guess I still want him to be proud of me."

"Oh, sugar, he certainly would."

He shook his head. "No, he'd be real disappointed. I'm disappointed in myself. I've caused so much hurt."

When Marabell saw the tears welling in his eyes, she grabbed him around his hefty waist with her short arms. "No, no, no. I won't let you do this to yourself. Nobody will even run against you. People in this town will always respect you. I'll make sure they do!"

"You can't *make* people respect you," J.P. said. "You have to earn it."

She turned him loose and pointed her finger in his face. "J.P. Jordan, you could not help this. Everybody knows that."

He looked at his mate of forty-two years. "No, Bellie. It's all my fault. Someday you'll see that." He turned away from her and watched the sunrise again. "I'd give anything if there was just some way to make this whole bad dream disappear."

Dye's Landing, Summer County   *May 30, 1998*

Ted was sitting outside his small cabin when Rocky's Tahoe pulled up the pine straw covered drive. He rose and walked over to the vehicle, surprised to see the game warden this early in the afternoon.

"I guess I should've been a reporter. You really get paid when you're sitting on your butt like that?"

Ted grinned. "Oh, yeah. Millions and millions."

"Look, I've got to run down to the dam for a couple hours. I asked Skeeter to come out and grill some burgers with me. Why don't you join us? She'll be out here around four. If you want to, go on over to my place and keep her company till I get back."

The prospect of seeing Skeeter away from the restaurant gave Ted a rush of excitement. He hoped to hell it didn't show. "Well, my social calendar is loaded this afternoon but I'll try to work this in."

"Yeah, right. Just make sure you two don't drink all my beer before I get there."

Ted hurried through a shower and even shaved. He had been waiting on Rocky's front porch half an hour when a blue Mustang rolled to a stop on the grass. He stood up as Skeeter slid out of the convertible and walked friskily up the front steps. She was wearing cut-off blue jean shorts and a sleeveless white blouse cut above her navel. *Damn, damn, damn. She shouldn't look that good!*

Skeeter paused on the top step and put her hands on her brown-skinned waist. "Hello, Mr. No-Menu, Coffee Black. So, Rocky stuck you with babysitting me."

Ted smiled. "Yeah, it's a tough assignment but somebody had to do it."

"Oh, am I that much trouble?"

"You look like trouble to me. I'm still trying to decide how much."

She gave him a phony frown. *Way too cute*, Ted thought.

He pointed to a rocker. "Have a seat Ms. Yates and I'll open Rocky's bar."

"So you're gonna wait on *me* now?"

"Yep. And in a private club like this, the tips are expected to be sky high."

She slowly rubbed her hands down each thigh, then extended her open palms. "Tips! Do you see any place I could be carrying money?"

Oh, man. I'd like to wake up beside her. He cleared his throat. "Okay, as long as you understand management reserves the right to strip search non-tippers."

She gave him a coy look.

"You wanna beer?" Ted asked. "We have a choice of Bud Light cold or Bud Light warm."

"I know. It'd be a miracle if Rocky ever had any wine or coolers. I'll just take a Bud."

Ted went inside the cabin and returned with two cold cans. Setting his down, he bent over and opened Skeeter's. She smelled so nice, more like clean soap than perfume. He plopped down in a chair beside her and opened his beer. She crossed her legs and got her rocker going full speed. Every little thing this woman did appealed to him. He watched her rock for a minute without speaking. "Have you ever considered leaving Summer?"

She planted her feet and halted the rocker. Her black eyes widened. "Well, no. Not really, I guess. I always figured everything I wanted was right here."

"So what do you want?"

She wrinkled her brow. "Well, I'd like a little family. A husband who was proud of me. A couple of kids and maybe a brick house in town."

Ted sipped his beer. "I don't understand why you don't have that. You would be a trophy catch for any man."

She blushed and looked away. "Maybe not anymore."

"Why not?"

"I'm not a young girl. I've already had my chances with two husbands."

"So why didn't you get the two kids and the brick house?"

She twisted her beer can in both hands. "I guess I really didn't wanna have Jake or Billy's child and they didn't wanna give me a house or anything else." Her dark eyes grew sad. "Maybe I shoulda tried harder." She sat her beer down and pointed with both hands to the corners of her eyes. "Look at these little wrinkles. They wasn't there a few years ago. It's just gonna get worse in a hurry. I'm gonna get up one morning and see that I'm too old to start a family with anybody. I worry 'bout getting fat and saggy in an empty house. I reckon it's my own fault."

Ted extended a long arm and patted her shoulder. "That's not the way I see it. Rocky Barnett should have been proud to have you years ago and he ought to be damn grateful for a second chance now."

She stared out at the lake. "I've 'bout given up on Rocky ever asking me. He's always known he'd get a yes."

Ted crushed his empty beer can. *Damn Rocky Barnett! He sure as hell didn't deserve to be this lucky.* "How about another beer?" She nodded yes and he ducked into the kitchen to retrieve fresh drinks.

Ted swung the screen door open with fresh beer in hand and almost hyper-ventilated. *Oh my God! What is she doing?* Skeeter was standing under the porch ceiling fan facing away from him. She had pulled her blouse up to the top of her small, round shoulders and was clawing away with both hands at a spot in the middle of her tanned back. "I love the scenery...but exactly what are you doing?"

"Them dog-gone chiggers! They always eat me alive out here." She kept her naked back exposed and started rolling her shoulder blades and wiggling her whole body under the fan's breeze. "I'm gonna just scratch this ole itch with air!"

He quickly sat the beer cans on the floor and walked toward her. "The least a gentleman can do is offer to scratch a lady's itch!"

He was just inches away from her when he heard Rocky's truck crushing gravel. *Damn it to hell, what lousy timing!* He heaved a deep sigh and retreated to his rocking chair to watch Skeeter squirm back into her top. Ted's pulse was still racing when Rocky climbed the front steps to the porch.

Over the next several hours, the three cooked venison burgers on a charcoal grill and shared another six-pack. Just before seven, Skeeter announced she was leaving. "You need to be careful on the road," Rocky said. "This morning a bunch of black guys were throwing rocks off the Warrior Bridge at any driver they thought was white."

"I'm just going out to mama's for the night," she answered. "I'll be there in fifteen minutes."

Rocky rose from the kitchen table to walk her out. She paused at the door and gave Ted a little wave. Ted smiled as his heart fluttered. *What a pisser. A woman like that in love with a man for twenty years who didn't even want her.*

Rocky came back to the table and sat down. He crossed his arms and looked at Ted. "You've asked me at least three times to take you to see Malachi Baines."

"That's right and you've said no once and hell no twice."

"Well, I've had my reasons. I didn't wanna go against J.P. and I'm not sure you can climb Piney Bald, but I've changed my mind."

Ted sipped his beer. "So now, all of a sudden, you think I've whipped myself into mountain-climbing shape?"

Rocky's demeanor remained somber. "I still have my doubts about that, but nobody has heard Malachi's side of the story. You could get it out. It might help calm things down. Too many people have already gotten hurt for no good reason...J.P. will just have to understand."

Ted shook his empty can. "If J.P. Jordan is fair and open-minded, he should *welcome* a chance to hear what Baines has to say. If not...your sheriff must have something to hide."

FOURTEEN

Associated Press Wire Service: Montgomery, Alabama   10:00 am   *June 1, 1998*

U.S. Attorney General, Diane Provo, and Alabama Attorney General, William Graddick, conducted a joint news conference outlining the federal-state cooperative efforts to end the impasse in Summer County. Provo announced U.S. attorneys had convened a federal grand jury to seek weapons law indictments against cultist Malachi Baines. Sources close to the investigation have told the A.P. that a local man will testify he witnessed a transaction near Summer where Baines received two military-style assault rifles in exchange for three sawed-off shotguns which he had illegally modified. Provo gave assurances that, once indicted, federal agents would proceed rapidly to apprehend and arrest Baines.

    Graddick said the state was close to completing its own investigation of the fatal dog attacks that claimed the lives of three Summer County deputies. The Alabama AG inferred that murder charges were imminent. He also said his office was working with Summer County officials in the ongoing investigation of the alleged molestation of Baines' teenage daughter. When questioned, Graddick emphatically stated his indictment and prosecution of Buck Yancey for the murder of Willie Gaddis would in no way hinder the pursuit of the murder case against Malachi Baines.

Cherokee National Forest, Summer County   10:30 am   *June 1, 1998*

His chest was burning with a searing pain. He gasped for air but could not suck it in fast enough. The roaring in his ears was deafening. Ted thought if he could breathe, he would puke his guts out. Rocky looked back at him. "I guess you need to rest again."

Ted let himself collapse belly-first onto the steep slope. His face plowed into the thick mat of decaying leaves on the floor of the wooded mountainside.

When his breathing slowed, he raised his head. "Damn, I'm loving this. I hope we have a lot more climbing."

Rocky grinned. "You're in luck. We still have about a mile and a thousand feet of elevation to go."

Ted rolled over and pulled himself into a sitting position as Rocky gestured toward the valley below them. "My daddy spent almost five years thinning the timber down there. Now you can't even tell it was ever cut."

Ted wiped his forehead with a dirty sleeve. "So your father's in the timber business?"

"He was killed in a sawmill accident when I was eight. But, yeah, he *was* in timber."

"Does your mother still live here?"

"Nope. She and my third stepfather live in Virginia."

"You have any brothers or sisters?"

"Yeah. I've got one sister. She's a school teacher in Jasper. A real small family. Mom left Summer with stepfather number two when I was in the ninth grade. J.P. was really the closest thing I ever knew of a dad."

Ted twisted around and looked at Rocky perched on a large rock. "You're almost like me. Not exactly a typical apple-pie family. So, why haven't you settled down with your own wife, two kids and a minivan?"

Rocky picked up a small stone and tossed it toward the vastness of the forest valley. "I don't know about families. I've never seen many that work. Two things happen when you don't make a commitment. You never have to worry about disappointing somebody and you never lose anybody you had planned on keeping."

Ted spat out some bits of leaves. "That's a crock. You also end up a selfish old man nobody gives a shit about. What in hell do you want to do? Do you plan to crawl around the woods busting frog poachers the rest of your life?"

Rocky hurled another stone. "I *could* stay happy right where I am…but I would like to be sheriff here someday. Not that it's a real possibility. J.P.'s probably got another ten years or so. Then most people will figure it's Spud's turn. I'd never run against Spud. By the time all the Jordans are through, I'll probably be too old."

"What is it about Summer? You could have a bright future lots of other places and your driving ambition is just to be the county sheriff?"

"I've had chances to leave. But you don't understand. Here, the sheriff, even the deputies, are looked at like heroes." A boyish grin crossed his face. "Actually, my first choice would be to roll back the clock and be the high school football captain again. Playing ball never felt as good at Auburn as it did here. Everybody knew you. Everybody patted you on the back, 365 days a year. Being sheriff in Summer County is a lot like that."

Ted struggled to his feet. "I can understand why you still want to be the homecoming king… Let's go. Malachi Baines may retire to Florida before I get the interview."

It took an hour to coax Ted another half-mile up the mountain. He needed a short break every ten minutes but now he had to rest longer. His sides were heaving and his clothes were soaked with sweat. When he could speak, he said, "I've been wondering about something. Why did the sheriff's department in this rural county have a SWAT team, and why would you try to make a climb like this wearing all that damn gear?"

Rocky was not even breathing hard as he chewed on a piece of grass. "The U.S. government. Last year the sheriff's department got a three hundred thousand dollar grant to train and equip a SWAT team. We all took some training and J.P. bought all the extra equipment. We even got GPS systems for five cars. You had to spend the money or lose the grant." Rocky took the stem out of his mouth and flicked it away. "They never intended to make this climb up the back side. Their plan was to cross Junee Bottoms where it's flat and go straight up the east face of Piney Bald. They would have only had to actually climb about five hundred yards. The real question is why they came up here in the first place...with or without SWAT gear. I guess I believe J.P.'s explanation...I just don't understand it." He unsnapped a canteen from his belt and tossed it to Ted. "Don't take but two more sips."

Ted nodded and gulped down the precious water. "Thanks. Are you worried about Baines detecting our approach?"

"Nope. They already know where we are."

"Are we in danger of being shot?"

"Malachi won't shoot me. I don't know about you."

"Great. How many snipers do *I* have to worry about?"

"You've been listening to too many reporters. There aren't any snipers. Nobody lives up here but Malachi, his wife Rebecca, his daughter Callie, two teenage sons and Rebecca's mother, Granny Tate. She's around eighty. They say she makes black magic but I don't think she's ever been a sniper."

"Are Baines and his sons armed?"

"Armed? They all survive by shooting game with .22s. That's not armed with very much." Rocky looked down at Ted. "You're all worried about the cult shooting you but you haven't said a word about all their attack dogs."

Ted grinned through the rivers of sweat on his face. "I figure I've earned some professional courtesy. One old dog wouldn't bite another one."

The two paused for Ted to rest one more time at the base of a jagged rock outcropping. "Damn, this is a long way up here," Ted gasped. "No wonder these people rarely go to town. How do the kids make it to school every day?"

"Zack and Jesse have already dropped out. Rebecca drives Callie down to Tate's Gap to catch the county school bus in the mornings and picks her up down there again in the afternoon. Come on, let's go. We're almost there."

They climbed a few more minutes, and then Rocky paused and whistled a two-note bird sound. The whistle was immediately repeated from the plateau above them. After another painful five minutes, Rocky pulled Ted by the arm onto the hard flat surface of Piney Bald. Ted bent over with his hands on his knees, wheezing desperately for oxygen. He slowly straightened up and blinked his eyes. He was facing a weathered unpainted building. A spotted dog with large floppy ears stood just a few feet away, sniffing the air curiously. Ted slowly turned his head to the left. A short bald man, with hands in his pockets, was staring at him as if he had just stepped out of a UFO.

"Ted Logan, this is Malachi Baines and that's Zack and Jesse." Ted then noticed the sons standing back behind their father. The two thin boys leaned against each other and shyly kept their eyes on the ground. Baines smiled, showing a mouth full of bright white teeth. He grasped Ted's hand firmly.

"Nice to meet ya. You don't look none too good. Come on up to the porch." Ted limped behind Rocky and Malachi. Baines and his kids looked so ordinary, middle-class even. No Grizzly Adams spitting tobacco through the gaps in his teeth. And not a gun in sight anywhere!

Malachi led the way up the front porch steps and gestured toward a cluster of crude but inviting cane bottom chairs. Ted noticed a pile of the bright orange FBI leaflets neatly stacked in the corner. He slumped into a chair and was immediately taken by the spectacular vista. The house overlooked boundless miles of green valleys and smaller hills. Two buzzards floated effortlessly in a clear blue sky. "Wow, this is quite a view."

Malachi rubbed the brown freckled skin on top of his head. "Yep, it's pretty up here. Next time, don't walk up so fast. You're looking green around the gills."

Ted touched his dry lips. "Yeah, I'll definitely walk slower next time."

"You want some water?"

"Yes, please."

"Zack, bring us a cold dipper." Shortly the older boy delivered Ted a well dipper full of cool, sweet water. He drank every drop without pausing.

"Thank you. I might live now."

Rocky grinned. "Ted's a reporter from Chicago. He doesn't get to climb many hills."

Malachi laughed as Ted wiped his mouth with the back of his hand. *This is truly amazing. Rocky's arrested Baines five times? Not a hint of animosity obvious with either man. They are sharing a joke at my expense like two close friends.*

Ted studied Malachi Baines. *Small man. Maybe five-eight or so. Late forties.* The remaining sandy hair that ringed his head was cut short and neat. His blue eyes were warm. He wore a short-sleeved denim shirt, faded jeans, and well worn work boots. His tanned face was fresh-shaven, even his fingernails were clean. Not at all the image Ted had built. No menacing giant in camouflaged fatigues brooding over the army gathered below his mountain.

"Chicago," Malachi said. "Do you know Paul Harvey?"

Ted raised his eyebrows. "I've met Paul on a few occasions but I don't know him well. Are you a fan of his?"

"I listen to his show every day I'm at the house. But I ain't liking what Mr. Harvey's said here lately." His small eyes brightened. "He's been calling my name but he's got the story all wrong. I'd like to send him a message."

Ted dug in his cargo pants and pulled out a notebook and tape recorder. "Maybe I can deliver your message. Will you talk to me on the recorder?"

"Sure. I done told Rocky last time if you was a friend of his, I'd trust you too."

Ted nodded. "Well, just tell me what you would like to say to Paul Harvey."

"He needs to know I ain't got no cult, no guard dogs or no AK-47s. It's just Becky 'n' me and the kids and Granny. I got three blue ticks and two catch dogs that won't even bite each other. An' they say they gonna arrest me for illegal weapons. I ain't never even bought a gun. I got my daddy's old 12-gauge and my uncle's .22. I ain't even got a real deer rifle. I traded for an aught-six a while back, but I done got shed of it." He cut his eyes at Rocky. "I don't hunt deer for sport, no way. The kids got a pair of .22s and a single-shot 20-gauge between 'em. We got enough ammo to feed us a few months. That's it."

Ted stopped his note taking. Malachi's sincerity was undeniable. "Have you ever owned dogs larger than one hundred pounds?"

"Ah, sha. I couldn't keep dogs that big fed. My hog dogs is 'bout sixty pounds. I got one tick maybe that big."

"I've seen a photo of you and your sons with your dogs and some dead pigs. It looks pretty gristly. Some people would say you and your sons participate in a brutal blood sport involving your dogs. How do you respond to that?"

"I don't know 'bout no sport. Hanging wild hogs in my smokehouse is 'bout not starving in the winter time. I'll get 'em any way I can. Them dogs help out a lot. If you is asking about wild critters dying to feed folks and bleeding out on the ground, I'd just say it's the way things work. Them hamburgers you eat down at McDonalds came 'cause a cow bled out hanging by its feet from a meat hook. Critters always bleed 'n' die to feed folks. Them wild hogs in that picture ain't no different."

"Do you know who might own the big dogs in Junee Bottoms?"

"Yeah, I reckon they belong to tha federal government. They done been in the national forest for years and years. I worry 'bout my hounds ever' time I run down there. I knowed something like this was gonna happen. Them dogs done got where's they ain't afraid of people no more."

"Mr. Baines, can you prove the Junee Bottom dogs don't belong to you?"

"I ain't got to prove that. I done told you they ain't mine."

Ted cleared his throat. "Sheriff Jordan has reason to believe your daughter Callie has been sexually molested. Do you know anything about that possibility?"

Malachi's face tightened. "I know what's being said. I ain't never laid a hand on my girl and I'd kill any man who wronged her." *The man's words were ringing true.*

"Has Callie hinted to you or her mother that an adult was assaulting her?"

"No sir. If she'd told us, the bastard would be feeding maggots."

"Do you *believe* anyone has hurt her?"

Baines squinted. "I don't reckon so. But Callie's at that age for gals. Going through all those things and all." A smile crossed his face. "Now she's ah filling out *real* nice! Making a fine looker of a grown woman...but she ain't talking much to me'n Becky. Just lays around most tha time, readin' and drawing those pictures. I reckon she talks to her Granny. Sleeps over there most ever' night."

"Do you think I could talk to Callie and her grandmother?"

"Now, I don't know 'bout that. Callie ain't gonna want to talk to no stranger and Granny won't even unbolt the door if'n she spots you in tha yard. No, I'm thinking that ain't no good idea."

Ted nodded. "The press portrays you as a convicted criminal. A repeat offender. Your record makes you an automatic suspect. How do you respond to that?"

"I ain't no criminal. If you's talking about that fight with Slick Hines, I was just defending myself. You can ask Rocky 'bout that. Now, me and Rocky get a little crossways every now and again. Ain't nothing to it. He's just doing his job. Sticking up for all them state rules. I'm just walking the woods trying to feed my family. I'm gonna do that. People gotta eat twelve months a year. Rocky knows how it is. We always work it out." He pointed toward Rocky. "This here's a good man."

"So you're contending all your game law violations occur as a result of providing food for your family?"

"I'm saying I do what I gotta do to take care of my own. Let me tell you something 'bout my people. In the depression, them rich bankers in Chicago and New York was jumping off buildings. Just quitting. That's tha easy way out. My granddaddy made whiskey and sold it for pennies. He didn't quit cause times was tough. He put food on tha table anyway he could. My daddy never knew times that wasn't tough. He never filed one of them bankruptcies nor left his family. When he had corn, he made whiskey. He trapped anything that walked, flied or swam and we ate every bite of it. But we never signed up for no welfare like them poor people in Chicago. That's tha stock I come from. I ain't no quitter and ain't gonna take nobody's handout. If'n that means I gotta shoot a deer in tha summer, I'm gonna do it. I only take just what I need. You can think that makes me a criminal but Rocky knows better."

"I understand what you are saying," Ted replied. "How will you and your family react if federal agents attempt to arrest you?"

"They ain't gonna arrest me for no made-up charges. If'n they try sumptin like that, I'd do what I gotta do!"

For the first time, Baines appeared agitated. He pointed at the tape recorder. "Cut that thing off." Ted clicked the button and obliged him. "Y'all gotta keep them feds from coming up my road. Rocky, you know I have a way to stop them tanks and trucks if'n I has to."

"Yeah, I know, Malachi. I'll do all I can."

Ted stood. "Mr. Baines, it would help my story and your cause if I could take a few photos."

"Sure, you just photo anything you wanna."

Ted pulled his digital camera out of a pants pocket. "I will need your help."

"I'll help you do anything you want."

"Okay, good. I'd like to photograph all the guns you own. Your dogs. A shot of you here on the front porch. Your sons."

With the help of Malachi, Zack and Jesse, Ted took over fifty shots. Rocky snapped several pictures of Ted petting the two scar-faced hog dogs.

Three hours after climbing out on Piney Bald, Ted and Rocky started back down. Fifteen minutes later, Ted needed the first oxygen break. He gulped in a painful deep breath. "Does it concern you that Malachi seems proud that Callie has developed a full figure?"

"Nah. It's just a mountain clan way of looking at their daughters. If they've got large breasts and round hips like Callie it means they're gonna be good baby-makers and the family will have an easy time marrying them off as young as possible."

Ted shook his head, "Well, to me, it sounds like a guy who's *at least* taking lustful looks at his daughter. And what did Malachi mean when he said he could stop the tanks if he had to?"

"I think I know. About a half-mile from his house, their private road passes the base of a steep rocky cliff they call Hawkeye Ridge. Malachi has access to dynamite and blasting caps from his cousins who work in the mines. He once told me you could bring the whole side of Hawkeye down on the road with a single blast. I think he could probably do that."

"So I assume that would block any vehicle passage until it was cleaned up."

"That's an understatement. If Malachi touched it off before they got to the pass, it could take five years to dig out the road. If he waited till they were in the pass, it could take just as long to find all the bodies."

FIFTEEN

The Monday, June 8th *Newslink* cover splashed the photo of a relaxed Malachi Baines leaning against his front porch rail with the panoramic Cane Ridge foothills as a backdrop. The bold headline above the picture read, **"Malachi Baines Tells His Story"** by Ted Logan.

"The law enforcement establishment has painted a red bulls-eye on the soft spoken father of three," Logan wrote. "Malachi Baines' survivalist lifestyle, proximity and past brushes with the law have made him the lone focus in the investigation of the dog-mauling deaths of four deputy sheriffs. The outcry for the justice of revenge overlooks the fact that the case against Baines is circumstantial at best and blatantly prejudicial at its worst." Ted related the details of his remarkable interview and Baines' denial of any responsibility for the dogs, ownership of illegal weapons or any improprieties involving his daughter. He painted the picture of a proud and fiercely independent woodsman whose life in a rugged environment was devoted to providing for his family. Ted went on to detail Malachi's reluctance to cooperate with federal authorities who blasted demands from helicopters that he surrender on unspecified charges. Rocky Barnett was quoted as saying Baines had no history of violent confrontations with arresting officers and his lone assault charge was, in fact, an act of self-defense. Ted revealed Rocky's own experience with a dog attack and the game warden's expert opinion that the killer animals were a long established pack of feral dogs.

Photos of Ted petting Malachi's hog dogs and holding Baines' two well-worn hunting guns accompanied the article. "The tragic loss of four officers has unleashed a torrent of emotions," Logan concluded, "An even greater tragedy looms if the assembled police force in Summer County persists in their rush to storm troop the home of a quiet rural family."

Dye's Landing, Summer County   *June 9, 1998*

Ted was sipping a hot cup of Bug Pepper's weed-killer coffee when three young men marched into the Sportsman's Bar and Grill. He sat down the heavy mug. *The feds. Cheap suits. Bad haircuts and an attitude you could spot a mile away. These three could be triplets if the guy on the right would lose his sunglasses.*

The middle agent briefly flashed a badge in Ted's direction. "FBI. I'm special agent Diamond and this is agent Stringfield and Donnelly. Mr. Logan, we need to ask you a few questions."

Ted took another drink of the stout coffee and winced at the taste. "Well, ask what you need to ask but don't count on getting answers."

Diamond's face flushed. "Were you with Malachi Baines the day of June 1st?"

"Oh, that one's easy. If you weren't too damn cheap to spend five bucks on yesterday's *Newslink*, you would already know I was."

The agent gripped the back of a chair until his knuckles turned white. "It is in your interest to cooperate with us. You crossed a police barricade to conspire with a federal suspect."

Ted laughed. "Yeah. It *is* one helluva barricade but I didn't see a single piece of yellow tape. Just pine trees and possums. And I think you'd better research your conspiracy theory. I believe it's on a collision course with the first amendment."

Diamond shoved the chair he was gripping, causing it to crash against Ted's table. "I've heard about you, Logan. You break the rules. This isn't a little street protest in Chicago. You can answer our questions or find it very difficult to continue covering this story. Who assisted you in getting to Baines?"

"You're right, Diamond, this is not a little protest in Chicago. It's a frigging police lynch mob. Who I see, who I talk to is none of your damn business. And unless you want your macho bullshit threat quoted in my next article, I suggest you and your skin-head mouseketeers get the hell out of my face." Ted calmly reached into his shirt pocket and laid his small tape recorder on the table.

Diamond reached for the machine, but froze when he realized Bug and two grizzled fishermen were intently watching him from the bar. He backed away from Ted's table and straightened his tie. "We *will* talk again soon, Logan."

Ted drained the last sip of his coffee. "Yeah, maybe next time you guys will be more forthcoming."

From his deep slumber in the still morning's early light, Ted was roused into semi-consciousness. His cell phone was ringing on the crowded nightstand. A booming voice with a southern drawl announced, "Mr. Logan, this is J. Riley Summer. You covered the '94 Luther Castleberry murder trial in Little Rock. I represented Mr. Castleberry."

Ted knocked the alarm clock and a stack of magazines off the small bedside table as he strained to retrieve his Camels and a lighter. "Yeah, I remember you." He lit a cigarette and pushed his back up on the headboard. "Castleberry filleted his wife and five kids with a hacksaw and you convinced the jury he was the victim."

Summer laughed. "Well, Mr. Logan, that case was certainly far more complex than your colorful summation."

Ted exhaled a cloud of smoke and rubbed his sleep-swollen eyes. "It didn't seem very complex to the grandmother who found all the fingers and eyeballs on the kitchen floor... but I have a feeling you didn't wake me up before daylight to reminisce about old times."

"No indeed, Mr. Logan. I am calling with an offer to represent Malachi Baines pro-bono."

"So why did you call me? I resigned as his agent last week."

"I know you have access to Mr. Baines. I have no other way to reach him."

Ted thumped ashes in the general direction of a packed ashtray. "So, the big name Houston attorney wants to jump into the dog-mauling spotlight. Aren't there any more Nazi prison guards to defend?"

"Actually, Mr. Logan, I have a personal interest in this case. I was born in Summer. My family goes back there a long way."

"No shit. You're one of the old general's descendants?"

"Yes. He was my great-great-grandfather. I left Summer to go to Yale and haven't been back."

"You know the sheriff down here?"

"Yes. My late father and J.P. Jordan were well acquainted…although I would not categorize them as friends."

"I see."

"Mr. Logan, I would be grateful for a few minutes of your time. My plane will be landing at the Coosa Track airport in about an hour. Can you meet me there?"

"Yeah, I suppose. If you promise to let me hold Castleberry's hacksaw sometime."

Cherokee National Forest, Summer County   *1:00 pm*   *June 11, 1998*

The cool rock felt good pressed against his clammy face. He hugged the boulder with both arms and drank in air in rapid gulps. *"Damn them both!"* Riley Summer had matched Rocky step for step without breaking a sweat. *Motor mouth attorney. Maybe he is getting a blister under his L.L. Bean hiking shoes.* Every time they paused for Ted to

117

rest, Summer railed on and on about the weak circumstantial case against Baines and the police over-reaction. Ted rubbed the sweat off his forehead with a soaked sleeve and looked up at Summer. The guy didn't look like a lawyer. Stylish cargo shorts, compass watch, safari hat, deep tan. The s-o-b could pass for a rock-climbing guide.

Rocky had seemed irritated the whole climb. Riley pointed at Rocky with his sunglasses. "Your testimony of your own experience with the feral dog packs will quash any murder indictments."

Rocky bit down hard on the short stick in his mouth. "I'm not real sure I should even *be* here. Much less testifying. If this was still just about the sheriff department's investigation, you'd be climbing up here without my help." He spat out the mangled twig. "It's only because the feds, the state, even the damn army rangers are hell-bent on blasting Malachi off his mountain that I'm bringing you to see him. But I still don't feel right about going behind J.P.'s back."

Riley snapped on his sunshades. "If your boss had properly handled this investigation in the beginning, none of us would be here!"

It was like the first time up the mountain. Rocky made a few birdcalls. Baines answered from the top. Then the excruciating climb was mercifully ended with Ted's burning knees collapsing to the mossy shale of Piney Bald.

Riley marched in the lead to the rustic front porch chairs and took a seat like he had been invited into someone's private office. He removed his hat and was barking out his war plan before Malachi, Rocky or Ted had even climbed the steps. "We have a team led by my senior partner working on the pending murder indictments. We will derail them in due course. My immediate concern is the weapons charges. They are currently the sole justification for the militaristic approach to your arrest. What is the nature of your relationship with James Isbell?"

Malachi leaned against the porch rail and cocked his head to one side as he studied the energized attorney. "I don't know you, mister. Rocky just sent word you was a lawyer come to help me. Heard you was a straight guy like this here reporter. I ain't got no money to pay no lawyer. I ain't broke no laws and I ain't sure why you is up here."

Riley nodded his head. "Okay, Mr. Baines, let me back up. I am J. Riley Summer of Summer, Baker and Watts. I have twenty-nine years experience as a criminal defense attorney and am offering to defend you pro – without charge. You obviously are in dire need of legal help. As an aside, I grew up here in Summer County. My father was John B. Summer."

Malachi scratched his leathery forehead and sat down in a rocker. "So you's from them Summers that the whole county's named for."

"Yes, that's right."

"Your daddy was that judge that tried to get J.P. Jordan kicked out as sheriff."

"My father was actually the district attorney for this county in the 1960s. And yes, at one point, he did investigate Sheriff Jordan."

"So how come you is willing to help me? You still out to get J.P. like your daddy was?"

"Mr. Baines, my father's legal encounters with Sheriff Jordan are ancient history. I assure you that has nothing to do with why I'm here. Mr. Logan can tell you that my firm has represented dozens of criminal defendants at no charge over the years. Your

119

situation is exactly the kind of case we seek out. Now. A Mr. James Isbell of Munfield has made some damaging statements concerning an alleged weapons transaction. Do you know James Isbell?"

Malachi nodded his head. "If'n James Isbell is the same as Jimmy Jack Isbell, then I know who he is. I bought my nine-month old tick bitch from him down in Munfield last year. Jimmy Jack's got some hounds with real good blood. Everybody knows that."

Riley raised his thick eyebrows. "Give me *all* the details of your dealings with Jimmy Jack Isbell."

"All the details is I give him fifty dollars and picked out a six-week old bitch pup."

"The transaction involved cash for a dog and nothing more?"

"That's right."

"Have you at any time had other business dealings with Isbell?"

"Nope. That's it."

"Isbell is currently under indictment for marijuana trafficking and possession of illegal weapons. Do you know anything about that?"

"I heard him and his brother growed crazy weed but that didn't matter none to me 'cause I knowed he had the best blue ticks around here." Malachi crossed his arms and rocked faster. "I seen them automatic rifles he had and them sawed-off scatter guns too. That's 'bout all I know."

"Mr. Baines, did you offer to buy or trade for any of those weapons?"

Malachi grinned. "Ah, sha. I ain't got no use for them big rifles and them shotguns is worthless. Cut off so short your pellets scatter a mile wide. You'd have trouble scratching a hog's belly at twenty feet with 'em."

"So you never received one of Isbell's weapons?"

"Nope."

"Have you ever modified a shotgun by sawing off the barrel?"

"Sha, I ain't ever had a shotgun I could waste that way. I done told this here reporter the onlyist two shotguns I ever had come down from my daddy's family. I sure wouldn't be sawing on my own daddy's 12-gauge!"

"The FBI has lifted your prints from a sawed-off shotgun found in James Isbell's home. Isbell has copped a plea bargain where he testifies that you modified several shotguns and traded them to him last fall for an AK-47 assault rifle."

Malachi clinched his jaw. "Well, Jimmy Jack is one lying sonofabitch. I ain't never cut off no guns and I ain't never got no assault rifle."

"So how do you explain your fingerprints on the confiscated weapon?"

"I looked at a couple of them short guns the day I got my pup. I picked 'em up and looked down the barrels. But I didn't do no trading of no kind 'cept to pay cash money for my pup."

Riley nodded. "They are squeezing Isbell to fabricate a story that would corroborate the circumstantial evidence of your fingerprints. Was anyone else present the day you bought the dog and examined the guns?"

"Preacher Jones was down there that day."

"Who is Preacher Jones?"

"I ran dogs with him for years 'round here. He's an old preacher man that lives over in Chalk County now. I heard he's got a little church and some new redbones over there."

Ted looked up from his scribbling. Riley Summer was neither recording the conversation nor taking notes. He studied the attorney's intense face. The guy was obviously brilliant. A legal genius with balls of steel. It was hard to like the fast-talking bastard's brassy personality. But, in real trouble, exactly the hard-ass lawyer you'd want at your table.

Summer spent another fifteen minutes in rapid-fire cross-examination of Malachi, and then jumped to his feet. "I have work to do, Mr. Baines. We will be in touch." The lawyer strode off the porch and out of sight behind the cabin before Rocky or Ted even stood.

Rocky looked at Malachi. "I guess your new attorney knows his own way home."

Chicago, Illinois   *12:00 noon*   *June 12, 1998*

Paul Harvey devoted two full segments of his syndicated program to updates from the galvanizing standoff in Summer County, Alabama. He concluded his broadcast with, "Malachi Baines. I hope you are listening today. Your fortunes have changed dramatically in recent days. You have had the opportunity to tell *your* story to the world through the nation's largest weekly magazine. And now, J. Riley Summer, arguably the top defense attorney in the United States who just happens to be the most famous native son of your own county, is representing you. J. Riley makes a compelling argument for

122

your innocence. Mr. Baines, you now have an opportunity for a safe and fair resolution to this sad saga. Please follow your attorney's advice and bring this unfortunate episode to a peaceful end for you and your family. We can only pray that the bloodshed in Summer, Alabama will now cease. This is Paul Harvey…good day!"

Summer, Alabama   *4:30 pm*   *June 12, 1998*

It was a meeting Rocky had been dreading all week. J.P. had Rita Jo radio him to come in to the sheriff's office on a game and fish day. Except for emergencies, the sheriff never intruded on his on-duty game warden shifts. Rocky anticipated a terse confrontation.

He hesitated at the glass door to the sheriff's private office. J.P. glared at him from behind the massive desk and gave a brisk wave of his arm for him to enter. He met the sheriff's icy stare and took a seat across from him without speaking.

"You've really surprised me, Rock. I expected better from you. You know this is the heaviest load I've ever had and the kid I practically raised is letting me down."

Rocky swallowed hard. "I'm sorry if you think I've let you down. I never want to do that. You're the man that taught me to follow my best instincts about right and wrong. I'm still trying to do that."

J.P. leaned back in his chair and cupped both hands behind his head. The tense grimace slowly disappeared from his craggy face. He sighed heavily and seemed to go somewhere far away. "Yeah, even as a little boy you had good instincts. I remember when you begged me not to take away Spud's bike after he purposely ran through Mrs.

123

Julian's flower garden. You said he would lose his paper route and not be able to pay for summer scout camp. You were right. He was a good kid too, and deserved a second chance."

The sheriff sat up straight and slowly stroked his chin. The old man's blue eyes looked sad, but no longer angry. "I know you've been guiding that reporter and now J. Riley up to see Baines. That's causing me a lot of static from the state and the feds. The press is pounding me 'cause I have a deputy that can walk right in there but we don't arrest Baines. And why didn't we use you the day of the raid? I point out that you are acting in your primary role as county game warden independent of the sheriff's department and in any event there is still no arrest warrant."

Rocky nodded. "We both know that's just a technicality."

"Yep, and we both know that once an arrest warrant *is* issued, your boss at game and fish will order you to make the arrest."

"I hope not, J.P. I guess we'll cross that bridge if it gets here. There should never *be* a warrant. I've said that from the beginning. I'm just trying to help an innocent man and not get anybody else hurt."

J.P. smiled a tired smile. "Rock, I know you mean that from the bottom of your heart. We don't see this the same way but I guess I'm glad a good man like you is taking the other side. I don't trust J. Riley. His old man was always out to get me." The sadness on his face deepened. "I've caused all of this grief. Off day or not, I know if we'd let you handle things back on the 19th, four good men would still be alive. I had my own reasons for what I decided that god-awful day."

Rocky stood and patted the sheriff's stooped shoulder. "J.P., that's all behind us now. We've got to move on and try to straighten out this mess. They've just about finished that damn steel monster of a bridge across Coon Creek. If the feds get a warrant, they will move up the mountain. Malachi only has a few more days to work with."

The sheriff stood and embraced the younger man. "Nobody really knows, son. A few more days is all any of us may have."

Piney Bald, Summer County   *12:00 midnight*   *June 13, 1998*

The thunder boomed in a cascade of explosions all around the high plateau. The jagged white lightning bolts streaked toward the dark forests far below the rocky peak. Inside the steamy old shack, a circle of homemade fat candles splashed orange light on Granny Tate's wrinkled face. The black-clad old woman held out a clutch of doll-like figures formed from corn shucks. Each crude figurine had a red star painted on its torso. She plunged the figurines into a pot of foamy brown liquid then faced the smelly candles and chanted, "Fire an' storm, wind an' rain. Kill them demon men that climbs my mountain! Drown their evil heads! Burn their foul guts in the fires of hell!"

SIXTEEN

Tate's Gap, Summer County   *June 14, 1998*

For seventy-two hours, a massive storm front stalled over north central Alabama. Parts of Summer County received ten inches of rain in less than two days. Streams and rivers rapidly swelled to flood stage. In the early hours of Sunday morning, June 14th, the soaking front finally moved to the east and blue skies reappeared over the green mountains. Federal agents mobilized at dawn to take advantage of the weather break.

On Saturday night, plans for the impending raid had leaked out to several news sources. CNN reporter Chet Hurdley and his camera crew made an early morning climb to position themselves as close as federal agents would allow to the Baines home. Hurdley made several live broadcasts from his post on the south side of the new Coon Creek bridge and was on the air again at 9:02 a.m. "Let me recap the recent events leading up to day twenty-seven of the Piney Bald standoff. On Friday, a federal grand jury indicted Malachi Baines on three firearm violations. Yesterday, in federal district court, Baines' attorney, J. Riley Summer, argued futilely for a halt to the imminent raid. Summer's contention that the indictment was flawed and the planned approach was needlessly forceful failed to sway a Birmingham judge. Summer's emergency appeal was still pending earlier this morning when U.S. Marshals decided to launch a large-scale raid to execute the federal arrest warrant at the home of Malachi Baines. At 8:00 a.m., approximately eighty U.S. Marshals, FBI and ATF agents left Tate's Gap in an armored column. The twenty-three urban assault vehicles moving north up this mountain weigh more than two hundred fifty tons. Alabama state police and FBI helicopters have been overhead all morning. I am here on the side of the winding muddy road that connects Piney Bald to Tate's Gap and the outside world. After more than an hour now, the column of agents have yet to cover the six miles to the point where I am standing. Just last Thursday the final obstacle to this military-style assault was eliminated. The Coon Creek bridge project was completed at a cost of over one million dollars. A new steel bridge now spans the four hundred feet across the Coon Creek gorge. Construction crews worked twenty-four hours a day for nearly three weeks to build the emergency bridge for the agents and their metal-plated machines. Late last night, field commanders decided all systems were go. It appears the Malachi Baines standoff is fast approaching a decisive, if heavy-handed, conclusion."

The CNN camera picked up the camouflaged Hummer that led the way onto the shiny new bridge. A gray tank-like vehicle followed close behind and then another Hummer. Hurdley gave his audience a play-by-play as the agents drove forward across the high suspension. "We can now see the lead vehicles rolling across the new bridge. It is indeed an eerie sight to see such fearsome machines in this spectacular wilderness setting. The lead vehicle is near the north bank high above..." A roaring crash drowned out Hurdley's voice as the camera captured the bridge suddenly collapsing in a surreal horror scene. "Oh, my God! Oh, my God! The bridge gave way! The bridge gave way! There is an avalanche of mud pouring down from both sides. Three, maybe four vehicles have completely disappeared. We can see only twisted metal down below in the muddy waters. Oh, my God!"

Summer, Alabama   *9:20 am*   *June 14, 1998*

J.P. and Rocky sat silently in the sheriff's office and stared at the small television set in the corner. The Fox reporter was talking against the backdrop of the Tate's Gap post office and general store. "Sources near the scene are reporting that ten or more federal agents are missing and feared dead after their vehicles fell over five hundred feet into a rain-swollen creek. A bridge recently constructed specifically for the agents' use apparently collapsed as their armored vehicles attempted to cross a narrow tributary known as Coon Creek. The agents were part of a large police force assembled to serve a federal arrest warrant on barricaded suspect Malachi Baines. It remains unclear if the bridge mishap was a weather-related accident or an act of sabotage by Baines and his followers. This incident happened only four miles northwest of the spot where four deputy sheriffs were killed on May 19th."

Rocky stood up and paced. "Sabotage! Their stupidity never ends! Malachi wasn't the cause of the bridge's collapse. It was probably ten inches of rain! If they had let us in the loop they would've known the road was too damn muddy for all that equipment. We hear about it on the news after they get a bunch of men killed! Damn them! Where will this madness stop?"

The old sheriff's hands were trembling. "It's my fault, son. I got four good men killed already. The feds don't want that kind of help."

"That's not true, J.P. If it's anybody's fault, it's mine. They know I can walk in Malachi's cabin anytime. They probably figured I would tip him off. They're so damn arrogant. Malachi knew they were coming the second they left Tate's Gap. We could've been a lot of help."

The older man turned his face away as tears rolled down his cheeks and dripped off his square chin. He sniffed and wiped his nose with the back of a large hand. "I'll never get over this, Rock. They say maybe ten more men died today. I caused all this. It hurts so bad."

Chicago, Illinois   *June 15, 1998*

The weekly Newslink cover featured an aerial photo of the Coon Creek disaster scene as rescue teams frantically searched for the missing agents. "Alabama Tragedy Grows" by Ted Logan was the lead headline. Ted's hastily revamped article recounted the events leading to the ill-fated raid that killed five agents and seriously injured four others. The piece went on to detail the intervention of J. Riley Summer and Malachi's account of his dealings with James Isbell.

Ted concluded: "The twisting and tragic drama in Summer County has now become the deadliest police episode in the nation's history. The public outcry for a decisive resolution is now deafening. In the twenty-seven days since May 19th, it has become evident that a puzzling decision by veteran sheriff J. P. Jordan triggered a shocking human disaster of growing proportions."

Rocky walked across Skeeter's cozy living room and slumped onto the padded

sofa. He rose up and pulled the TV remote control from under his bottom and pushed the

'on' button. The Fox News Channel had a panel of experts discussing wild dogs in the

United States. "Many such feral populations have been well documented for decades.

As an example, a particularly distinct sub population has long been known to exist in

parts of South Carolina. The so-called "Yellow Dogs" of South Carolina are believed to

have been established for over a century. The Carolina wild dogs have evolved into a

uniform body confirmation and distinctive light tan coloration, hence the "yellow dog"

nickname. They have become largely nocturnal and have assumed many of the hunting

patterns and pack social structure of native wild dogs such as wolves and coyotes.

Likewise, there are many other known feral packs throughout the Southeastern and

Appalachian states…including eastern Alabama."

"But Dr. Kimber," the moderator interrupted, "is there any record of human

attacks by these various wild dogs?"

"Yes. In fact, since 1980, I know of at least 25 such incidents resulting in three

deaths prior to the recent attack in Summer County Alabama. Feral dogs are large

aggressive territorial predators. Worst of all, unlike indigenous wild canines, they have

no instinctive fear of man."

Rocky had heard enough. He clicked off the TV, leaned back on the sofa and

momentarily closed his tired eyes. A sweet familiar smell drifted into his consciousness.

It always made him think of fresh honeysuckle blooms. He felt Skeeter's nimble fingers running through his rumpled hair. She always smelled so intoxicatingly nice. He opened his eyes and stared at her pretty face.

"You look so sad Rock. This is all so awful for you. Your buddies got killed. Now these Marshal guys too."

He looked deeper into her dark moist eyes. "It's been tough as hell Skeet."

She gave him that special smile that always warmed his soul. "You want some cheese or something?"

"Yeah, I'll take the 'or something'."

She slid off the couch and kneeled at his feet. Her slender fingers playfully removed his bulky police belt then probed inside his pants. She worked his zipper open and buried her head between his legs as he winced with enjoyment. Over and over her head bobbed as his pleasure intensified. He slid the fingers of both his hands deep in her thick mass of shiny hair and climaxed in a moan of ecstasy.

Seconds later, he clutched her in a bear hug on the old sofa, stroking her glimmering hair as he gasped for breath. "You're so sexy baby."

She kissed his thick sweaty neck. "It's 'cause you make me feel that way."

He squeezed her even tighter. "I know I haven't done you right. I…I still don't know what I want to do Skeet. I'm uh…I'm uh little afraid of getting old and dying alone. Hank and Lem and all of them getting killed makes you think…but I just can't seem to…you know…get married or anything."

She looked into his somber blue eyes. "Rock baby, I ain't going nowhere as long as you want me to stay. 'Cause I reckon I could just always wait 'till you know for sure."

He hugged her again. "If I could ever do it, you'd be the only one I'd ever do it with."

She kissed his forehead. "I know that Rock...Rock you don't think I'm too old to marry do yah? I sag a little here now and these crowsfeet are..."

He pressed a finger over her lips. "Shhh. You're still so nice to look at. You're a real prize of a woman any man would be glad to have."

"But Rock, you don't think I'm too damaged...or used up to marry do yah?"

He took her hand and held it. "There's nothing wrong with you baby. I guess I'm really the one that's got all the warts and dents."

Locust Fork Road, Summer County   *11:30 pm*   *June 17, 1998*

Ted gripped the dashboard as the Tahoe pulled out of another rut. "So why in hell are we bouncing our asses in the middle of the night looking for damn poachers? We're right here on top of the biggest police story in thirty years and you're trying to pinch a Bubba for shooting a deer!"

Rocky roughly shifted into four-wheel drive. "It's my damn job! There's not a damn thing I can do about the Baines investigation. I need to get away from all the fed's bullshit. And you can crawl your butt out on the road if you don't like what I'm doing!"

"This is *not* a road. Roads have asphalt and stop signs."

The game warden shifted gears again and sped up. "Why are you so damn cranky? You always carry a chip on your shoulder. You're a big shot reporter with a big shot reputation. You're getting your damn story just like you always do. So why don't you back off my tail?"

Ted lit a cigarette and exhaled toward his half-opened window. "I don't always get my story and I learned a long time ago what it's like to get screwed out of a story. I've never had the luxury of backing off anybody's tail."

"So what does that mean?"

Ted glanced at his young companion. "Something big, very big, happened in American politics in the early 70s...I'm sure you were too young to remember."

"Try me. I actually learned to read at an early age."

Ted sucked in deeply on his cigarette and exhaled as he spoke. "You ever read about Nixon and Watergate?"

"Sure...the break-in, the cover up – All of that stuff."

"Well kiddo, I cracked that story. I had a reliable source that fed me the first leaks."

"Yeah? I always thought those two Jewish newspaper guys were first to crack that."

"The whole damn world believes that...but Watergate was *my* story. My baby. My bestseller, my Pulitzer. A guy I thought was my best friend screwed me over for a few bucks and stalled me going to press with his bullshit lies." Ted thumped his cigarette butt out the window. "If I've got a chip on my shoulder, it's because I *know* how the frigging world works."

The bouncing headlights illuminated the rear of a parked vehicle. Rocky immediately killed his lights and shut off the engine. "That's them. They're probably butchering what they've shot down in Oden's Hollow. Maybe on the Jordan place. I guess you can tag along behind me if you stay quiet and hit the ground, flat on your belly, when I give you the signal. I can't guarantee you won't get shot and if you do, I'm gonna leave your Chicago ass in the woods."

"Let's go. Don't worry about *my* Chicago ass. If I get whacked down here, at least I've enjoyed all the fried chicken."

Fifteen minutes later, Ted was struggling to keep up as he rubbed another itching mosquito bite on his sweaty arms. The salty taste on his lips told him the last branch that slapped his face had drawn blood. Rocky was moving through the shadowy woods ahead of him like a large cat. Silent and agile, he paused often, then moved ahead with short, deliberate steps, stalking his prey in the darkness.

They crept through a stand of large trees and froze at the edge of an opening in the forest. Rocky waved his hand for Ted to get down. Ted obeyed the command and propped on his elbows to watch. *How the hell does he do it? Never hits a limb. Never even rustles the leaves. The guy must have night vision and foam rubber feet.*

The game warden moved forward a few more feet and pressed his chest against the trunk of a large tree. Ted could smell a strong putrid odor and hear muffled voices. Rocky slowly detached a flashlight from his police belt and pulled his gun from its holster. Holding the light in his left hand, he stretched his left arm as far as he could around that side of the tree. He looked around the right side of the tree and pointed his weapon with his right arm.

Holy Crap! He's extending his light so they'll shoot at him too far to the left! Ted felt a rush of adrenaline when he heard the safety click off.

Rocky flicked on the flashlight and shouted, "Freeze, assholes! You're under arrest!" There was a short tense silence, then Rocky shouted again. "Joe, they're going to run. Turn loose the dog!" When a growling bark came out of the game warden's mouth, Ted thought he would pee his pants.

Ted heard crashing sounds, then "Don't turn them dogs loose! We ain't going nowhere!"

Rocky answered, "Stand still and drop your guns. Do it now!" He waited for the poachers to comply. "Now, walk toward this light a few steps. A little closer. Now, get down on your knees. Both of you! Now! Now, lay flat on the ground. Flat, I said! On your belly!" Rocky moved away from the tree and slowly approached the men. He kicked one man's leg. "You...crawl around and lay head to head with this other one. Don't get up! I said *crawl,* dammit! You want the dog to chew your butt?" When the two men were laying head to head with their arms stretched out, Rocky pounced on top of one and quickly cuffed his hands behind his back, never taking his eyes off the second man. In mere seconds, he reversed positions and cuffed the other man.

Ted raked leaf fragments out of his hair and stood up. Rocky was picking up rifles and walking around the scene. "You guys have had a busy night. Two does and a fawn. Congratulations. That's worth your guns, your truck, two thousand dollars and ninety days."

The taller suspect twisted on the ground and looked up at Rocky. "Where's your partner and them dogs?"

"Don't worry about them. What you need to worry about is this reporter here with me. He's a trained killer."

The guy coughed and spat. "You's Barnett, ain't you?"

"That's right."

"The onliest reason we is out here tonight is 'cause your boss is selling out."

"What the hell are you talking about?"

"J.P. Jordan and his cousin Bobby Dees owns this here piece of land and they's selling it to these Birmingham guys. They's gonna cut the trees and run off all the deers."

"Are you a real estate agent now? I haven't heard that J. P. was selling."

"It's a fact. Bobby says J.P.'s done got hisself in real bad money trouble."

SEVENTEEN

---

81 World Trade Union Building   Chicago, Illinois   8:30 am   June 18, 1998

Susan Rollins leaned forward and pushed a button on her desktop speaker phone. "Hello, Ted. Your story keeps growing new legs by the day!"

"Yeah Susan, it does. I'm still not sure where all this is heading…but it's unfolding fast. I'm at a point where I need some help. I have a new angle on the sheriff, J.P. Jordan. Apparently he is experiencing some financial problems. I need some specialized expertise. Can we retain the Forensic accountants from Baltimore to trace all of Jordan's financial affairs?"

The Newslink editor did not hesitate. "Sure Ted. I will have Benjamin Golden call you this afternoon. Ted, there is something I've been meaning to tell you. I've watched you grow as a journalist for nearly 30 years. You have always had an uncanny knack for digging to the bottom of a complex story. My instinct tells me when all the dust settles in Alabama, this assignment will be a career story for you and a real coup for Newslink. Anything you need from me, you've got!"

A three judge panel of the 11th Circuit Court of Appeals has ruled in favor of a motion filed by Malachi Baines' defense attorney. The unanimous decision by the judges in effect squashes the weapons charge indictments previously upheld by a lower Federal Court and places in question the validity of federal search warrants ATF agents have been attempting to serve on Baines at his remote home near Tate's Gap Alabama. The panel was swayed by the testimony of the reverend Wilburn D. "Preacher" Jones who contended that he witnessed the events that lead to Malachi Baines' fingerprints being lifted from an illegally modified shotgun belonging to convicted felon James Isbell. The appeals court ruled that the district court judge and the grand jury had failed to consider Rev. Jones' exculpatory statements. Lead Baines attorney, J. Riley Summer, in a post-decision press conference noted what he called "the greatest of legal ironies." Earlier in the day, prosecutors in Alabama convened a new federal grand jury to consider murder charges against Malachi Baines for the alleged "bridge sabotage" deaths of five federal agents. Only hours later, the 11th Circuit rejected the validity of the arrest warrants the agents were attempting to execute when they lost their lives.

Birmingham, Alabama   *5:30 pm*   *June 18, 1998*

"Damn rush hour traffic." Rocky grumbled from the passenger seat of Ted's rental car.

"You should see Chicago traffic at 5:00 in the afternoon," Ted replied as he adjusted his sunglasses. "This little I-20 slowdown's not bad." The bumper sticker on the van in front of them caught Ted's eye. "Back off or I'll turn you into a frog." Ted chuckled. "Do you think she's a graduate of the Tate's Gap Institute of Black Magic?"

Rocky did not seem amused. "I'm not real sure you should just laugh all that off."

"You're kidding me! The great tailback and fearless peace officer really buys all that voodoo nonsense?"

"I'm not saying I buy all of it, but I've lived around those hill clans all my life. I've seen enough strange happenings to at least wonder if the old mountain witches can cast a spell. It's like spotting a stick on the trail in front of you and wondering if it really is a rattlesnake. It would be pretty foolish to step on top of it before you knew for sure it *wasn't* a snake. I wouldn't want to piss off Granny Tate or old Aunt Lizzy Haines. Those old gals have a special knowledge and maybe a power that most of us can't even comprehend."

Ted shook his head in disbelief and changed the subject. "Tell me about Brad Cowan. So, you've known him since college. He's been with the Alabama Bureau of Investigation for ten years. Why is he so willing to buck his superiors and talk with us secretly about this investigation?"

A sly grin crossed Rocky's face. "It's because I *asked* him to. We go way back. Brad has a beautiful wife of 15 years, a filthy rich father-in-law, two great kids, a big house, and a great job. Once upon a time on a dark night in Auburn, Alabama I saved that whole damn dream life for him. He won't ever forget that!"

Thirty minutes later, the two men walked into a quaint bar off Birmingham's Five Points South and met Rocky's old friend. "Ted Logan, let me introduce you to Brad "Boomer" Cowan, All SEC Safety and ABI agent extraordinaire!"

Ted took the slim built man's firm handshake.

"Yeah, I'm still amazed about that All SEC part. It came in an era when wide receivers had lighter complexions, were slower and a lot easier to cover! I'd be lucky to make the scout team at Auburn in today's game."

Ted chuckled. "It sounds like you're an all-star at the ABI these days."

139

Brad's smile disappeared and his forehead wrinkled into a frown. "The agency is very political. The real ABI all-stars are good at kissing the right politician's ass. The Summer County investigation is being directed by one of Governor Allen's ABI "yes men." The Governor's Chief of Staff calls the shots almost hour by hour." Brad looked down at his foam capped beer mug and rubbed his eye brows with his right index finger. "There is no viable evidence to support a murder indictment for the three deputies' deaths…but the Governor and the AG keep pushing us to build a case for indicting Baines." The agent raised his head and looked Ted in the eyes. "The AG is even more damned determined to prosecute Buck Yancey for Willie Gaddis' death."

Rocky cleared his throat. "Buck's slug in Willie's chest is hard to refute, but what about the slug in the white dog's head – why no ABI ballistics test?"

Brad reached inside his sport coat and pulled out a thick folded set of papers. "It's all in here. There *was* a ballistics test and the bullet in the white dog was not fired from Buck's gun. – It was matched to Dave Ellis' Glock!"

Rocky pounded the table. "Damn! And how many rounds were missing from Ellis' piece?"

Brad flipped a page of the folded report and read silently a few minutes. "Two. There were definitely only two rounds fired. It is assumed Ellis used the other round to kill the black dog latched onto him at point blank range."

"But no slug was recovered from that dog?"

"No, the only slug found in any dog was Ellis' bullet in the white one."

Rocky put a hand on his friend's shoulder. "A bullet fired into the black dog that close would probably have passed clean through him. It's buried up in the ground at the scene. We've got to recover that slug. Can you do that Brad?"

The slim man slowly nodded his head. "Yes I can. Getting the assignment will be easy enough. I'll have to be real careful what I do with the results."

"I'll bet," Ted replied, "It sounds like the brass at the ABI choose to ignore any evidence that doesn't fit their agenda."

"Exactly right. Our director is so tight with Graddick, I think they're sharing saliva. The reason we are still sitting on the ballistic match from the white dog is because the AG doesn't want to compromise his case against Yancey until after the election. The black vote in this state *is* 30% after all!"

Rocky locked his hands and popped his knuckles. "If you can help us Boomer, we *will* get to the bottom of this."

Associated Press Wire Service: Summer Alabama   11:25 pm   June 20, 1998

Local news sources are reporting the Westville home of Bertha Langham has been destroyed by a fire of suspicious origin. Bertha Langham, 39, is the mother of Clenzo Langham, 22, currently being held in the Summer County jail on murder charges stemming from the May 26 shooting death of Josh Thomas, 21, of Summer. Ms. Langham shared the home with Clenzo and four younger siblings. Racial tensions in the area have escalated further since the death of Thomas, who is white, in a bar room gun battle between groups of white and black men. There are no reported injuries from the fire. The Summer County Sheriff's Department is investigating.

June 22nd Newslink copies hit the newsstands with a fourth straight cover featuring the conflict in Summer County. A photo of Alabama Governor, Bog Allen, standing on the Summer courthouse steps with a clenched fist raised toward the media was under Ted Logan's headline title "The Politics of Summer Siege."

"The popular appeal of brute force police action has proven irresistible to politicians from Montgomery to Washington. Alabama incumbents locked in tight election year races, as well as the Clinton Whitehouse, have seized on the Summer County tragedies to shamelessly milk the raw emotions of revenge."

The article revealed that both Governor Allen and Alabama Attorney General William Graddick were trailing their general election opponents in May. A month's worth of charged rhetoric directed at Malachi Baines had given both Alabama politicians huge jumps in the polls.

Ted relayed the evidence of the Governor's direct involvement in the day to day conduct of the state's investigation. A Newslink national poll taken on May 1st found that 61% of Americans viewed the Clinton Justice Department as soft on crime. U.S. Attorney General, Diane Provo, had devoted five press conferences in 30 days to the Tate's Gap operation. Ted concluded, "The political demagoguery centered on the Baines family overlooks many flawed assertions surrounding the deaths of four Summer deputies and five federal agents. An isolated rural family has quickly become hapless scapegoats for politicians of every stripe. Only time will tell if opinion polls and pending elections lead to the spilling of more blood in the mountains of East Alabama."

EIGHTEEN

Summer, Alabama   *9:50 am*   *June 22, 1998*

Rocky hesitated as he walked by Rita Jo's work station and overheard a 9-1-1 operator relaying an urgent request for assistance. "There's a gang assault in progress in the Westville Citgo parking lot. At least one victim is down on the pavement, bleeding. A store clerk reports a group of black males are beating two white guys with baseball bats."

Rita Jo keyed her radio, "D-23, R-20, D-1, D-4, Code 3 to Highway 60 Westville Citgo. 10-10 in progress with injuries. All units report 10-20's and stand by. EMT units to follow sheriff's dispatch."

J.P. walked briskly up to Rocky and tapped his shoulder. "Come ride with me Rock." He glanced back at the dispatcher. "I've got the ball on this one Rita Jo."

She nodded and transmitted the order, "S-1 and R-12 Code 3 from base. S-1 has the point."

As the sheriff's car sped out of town, Rocky looked closely at J.P. He was driving near 80 miles per hour with one hand on the wheel and barking out instructions into his mic. "D-23 secure the scene, but do not pursue suspects 'til back-up arrives." The sheriff looked energized, confident and in control, like his old self.

143

Rocky adjusted his seat belt. "J.P. you know this is going to push the whole county over the edge."

The sheriff seemed totally focused on the crisis at hand. "I'll get the state to set a perimeter on Highways 19 and 60. We're calling in all shifts, all reserves. I want Jocko to get the second and third shift mobilized in riot gear." J.P. drew a deep breath, "Rock, when this is done, I want you and Spud to go with me to see those two black preachers over there. We're gonna get this situation calmed down." Rocky nodded his head. This was the J.P. Jordan he had always known, strong and prepared, but level-headed and pragmatic.

At 10:17, the sheriff's car squealed into the Citgo parking lot. Rocky immediately spotted a young white man sitting on the asphalt leaning back against the rear tire of a grey Honda Civic. The teenager appeared to be in shock as blood drizzled from a long gash in his cheek. Rocky pulled out his handkerchief and pressed it tight against the open wound. "Hey Buddy, you're gonna be all right. Just stay still. Help's on the way." He gently raised the boy's left hand up to the bloody cloth. "Here, hold this on your face. Press real hard. Can you keep this pressed tight?" The young man nodded. "Good. Okay. I'll be right back. Just keep pressing tight."

When Rocky stood up, he heard Spud call out from the opposite side of the Honda. "I've lost his pulse! I've lost his pulse!" He dashed around the car and found the chief deputy kneeling over another youngster whose bloody face was bashed beyond recognition.

"We'll bring him back Spud! You pump his chest. Start pumping his chest. Now! You can do it. You can do it!" Rocky tilted the boy's bruised chin up and stuck

144

two forefingers back into his throat. As he pulled his swollen tongue out of his blocked airway, Rocky's fingers raked broken tooth fragments out of his mouth and onto his ripped shirt. As gently as possible, he squeezed the boy's battered nostrils tight with his left hand and locked his own mouth over the young man's cracked lips and blew air into his lungs. He blew in, covered the boy's mouth with his right hand and blew in again and again with an up and down rhythm.

"Good Spud, Good! Keep it up, keep it up!" After a few anxious minutes, the boy's body suddenly jerked in a violent convulsion that caused Spud to rock backward onto his heels. When the teenager made a gurgling cough, Rocky quickly rolled him onto his side and with his bare hand, wiped the reddish dribble away from his open mouth. The boy wheezed loudly and spit up more bloody phlegm. Rocky could hear the first rescue unit rolling in behind him. "He's breathing Spud! He's gonna make it!"

Within seconds the EMTs took over and started administering oxygen. When Rocky stood up, J.P walked over and patted his shoulder. "Good work son. Real good work. You and Spud pulled the kid through. Maybe he's out of the woods. Now let's see if we can round up the thugs that did this. The clerk inside has identified two of 'em by name."

Twenty minutes later, J.P. and Rocky led a five car police caravan down a narrow, pot hole riddled street in north Westville. The homes clustered on both sides of the broken pavement were a hodge-podge assortment of rusty trailers and small poorly built frame houses of various configurations. Small groups of black people were gathered in nearly every yard. None were smiling and most glared at the passing police convoy. Three young men shouted and made angry gestures from a front porch.

J.P. stopped his cruiser in front of a crumbling half-house built onto a sky blue mobile home. He glanced at Rocky and spoke firmly into his radio, "D-1, D-4, D-23, take positions in the back yard. State police back us at the front door and cover the front flanks."

Car doors flew open and eight officers rushed around the weedy, garbage-strewn yard with weapons drawn. Rocky pulled out his Glock and walked shoulder to shoulder with the sheriff across the cluttered yard and up the rickety front steps. Hickory scented smoke from a neighbor's home-made barbeque grill wafted across the wobbly front porch.

J.P. looked at Rocky and grinned, "Those ribs sure smell good." He drew his own weapon and calmly approached the front door. "Let's just see if those two Jackson boys are home."

Rocky raised his gun with both hands and assumed a coverage position facing the swing side of the door.

J.P. rapped hard three times on the flimsy aluminum door causing the loose glass panes in the top of the door to rattle. "Sheriff's department. Open up!" There were no discernible sounds from inside the structure. He banged loudly again. "Sheriff's department! Open the door or we're coming in!" After a brief pause, the sheriff nodded at Rocky, lifted his right leg and gave the shaky door a firm kick.

The door caved in so easily that J.P. stumbled forward into the opening. Rocky wheeled into the house with his weapon pointing and his eyes darting toward every corner of the messy front room. The windows were all covered with tacked-up bath towels. Only the light pouring in from the open front door illuminated the piles of soiled clothing and tattered furniture.

The sheriff caught his balance and took a halting step forward. "Anybody in here? Answer me!" The room was sticky hot and smelled of beer and stale cigarette smoke. J.P. took another tentative step to his left toward an open interior door. Just as Rocky lunged forward to cover the open hallway door he heard a faint bumping noise and smelled the unmistakable odor of adrenaline drenched human sweat. At that moment, the sheriff who was a step closer to the doorway inched forward as Rocky instinctively grabbed for his shoulder. "J.P. wait!"

A single gunshot shattered the tense quietness. Rocky saw the bright orange shotgun muzzle blast a millisecond before J.P. was knocked violently backward smashing a small table as he fell. Rocky fired four quick rounds down the shadowy hallway and screamed, "Drop the gun, drop the gun!" He pressed his body against the wall to the left of the door opening and keyed his mic "10 double zero, 10 double zero, S-1 is down! We've gotta 10-32 in the back hall of the house. He may or may not be hit!"

Spud took command in the backyard and ordered two deputies to surge forward to positions on either side of the back door.

Rocky strained intensely to see around the corner over his handgun barrel. *He was so torn! J.P. was still and silent. He had to get to him quickly! There were no sounds from the hallway. Was the shooter dead or waiting again in ambush?*

Spuds high-pitched voice came over the radio. "R-12, R-12 give me your status. We're in place to knock in the backdoor!"

Rocky swallowed hard, "Knock it down D-1. I'll try to give you inside cover."

Frank Lipscomb quickly pried open the backdoor with his pocket knife and Sam Gibson rolled his lanky frame onto the rear bedroom floor. With the burst of sunlight from the open backdoor, Rocky could now clearly see a motionless man slumped against a wall ten feet down the hall. An automatic shotgun lay on the floor beside the man. He gripped his Glock tighter. "Show me your hands damn it! Show me your hands!" He cautiously stepped into the hallway. The crumpled figure never moved. Rocky crept forward and kicked the shotgun away from the man's limp body before gripping his blood-soaked neck. *No pulse.* "10-32 is down and out. There may be more people in the back. Be careful!"

As Frank Lipscomb crawled into the bedroom behind Sam Gibson, a closet door in the room popped open and two young black men sprang out and dashed toward the open back door. Gibson swung his gun around to cover the men and shouted, "Stop! Stop!"

When the first teenager tried to duck around Lipscomb, the burly sergeant still on his knees and holding his gun in one hand, grabbed the boy's leg with his other large hand and wrestled him to the floor. Gibson jumped to his feet and tackled the second boy from behind with such force that he drove him out through the open door and face first onto the splintery back porch. The other deputies and state troopers surged in to handcuff the pair and sweep through the house.

Rocky turned from the downed gunman and dashed to J.P.'s side. The big man, pale and deathly still, lay at a contorted angle atop the broken coffee table pieces. *Oh God please no, please no!* Rocky ran his trembling hands rapidly over the sheriff's limber

148

body. *Lots of blood everywhere – but he's still breathing! Thank God! His vest took most of the buckshot, maybe just a knock out lick when his head hit the table.* He twisted his head toward the radio microphone clipped to his shoulder. "D-1 the Sheriff's alive! Get the EMTs rolling!"

Within seconds Spud raced into the dusky room and dropped to his knees beside his prone uncle. Kneeling beside Rocky, the chief deputy placed his right hand under the sheriff's neck and gently supported his head. With Sam's help Spud and Rocky eased J.P. down off the busted table and on to the greasy carpet.

Frank angrily ripped a faded towel off a window. "Tha bastards had it so damn dark in here you can't see squat!" The deputies carefully removed the sheriff's pellet riddled protective vest and his uniform shirt.

Spud gingerly lifted his blood soaked undershirt. "I think he's okay Rock. It looks like just two or three pellets got around the vest. All that blood came from these two holes in his arm. He's just bruised up real bad and probably got a concussion."

Frank Lipscomb walked over and nudged the shooter's body with his foot. "You nailed the s-o-b hard! At least two in tha chest and one right 'n his throat. He woulda killed you both if you didn't get him when you did."

Sam gripped J.P.'s ankles and lifted up both his feet. With his legs elevated, the color slowly returned to the sheriff's deeply lined face. He wrinkled his forehead and blinked his eyes. "I guess I make too big ah target," he said weakly.

Spud squeezed his hand. "Don't try to talk just yet J.P. We're gonna get you on tha wagon and rolling out of here. You're gonna be fine."

J.P. blinked again to try and clear his foggy vision. "Look Spud. Now you and Rocky have to go to those black preachers. It's more important now than ever. Go see Ole Brother Terrell first and tell him I sent you. We gotta do what we can to settle all this down." The shrill sound of approaching sirens penetrated into the cramped musty living room.

South Westville   *5:00 pm*   *June 22, 1998*

Rocky and Spud pulled into the gravel driveway of the modest white-sided house. The small yard was trimmed and neat. There were seven black men sitting or standing on the wide front porch. The well-dressed group watched in silence as the deputies climbed the freshly painted front steps. Spud approached a small dapper white-headed man seated in an oak rocking chair. "Good afternoon Brother Terrell. I appreciate y'all seeing us." The little preacher nodded somberly and shook Spud's hand. "Brother Terrell, I'm sure you know Rocky Barnett."

The preacher gave a faint smile. "Oh yes. Me 'n' Rocky go back a ways." He took Rocky's hand. "I axed de deacons to join with us today." The deputies then shook hands all the way around with the front porch delegation.

Spud cleared his throat, "Brother Terrell, J.P. was planning to meet here with you today, but after he got shot, he asked me 'n' Rocky to speak with you. We all feel bad 'bout all this violence and hard feelings between tha black folks and tha white folks. J.P. was hoping you and your church could work with tha sheriff's department to try and calm things down."

150

Brother Terrell nodded and rubbed his cotton beard. "J.P. Jordan is a fine gentle man. He's been fair to our peoples hiss whole life. In 1965, J.P. Jordon was de only sheff in Alabama who refused to attack de black folks who was machin to Selma. We hopes and prays de sheff's gonna make it through his injury." He gestured toward the deacons circled around him. "De problem for our peoples is...yet another black man is dead." He looked Rocky steady in the eyes and continued in his soft tone, "I knows dat Rocky had no choice. Leroy Jackson tried to kill de sheff. Leroy had evil in hisself to shoot de sheff. Some of our peoples will say Leroy was jest protecting hiss own nephews in hiss own house...but I knows dem boys was wrong to beat up dem white boys and I knows de sheff 'n' Rocky was jest doing deys job...but our peoples is hurting and mad and dey's scared. All de's outside hot heads got 'em riled up." The preacher paused and looked solemly at the deputies, "But with tha' Lawds help, we's will do what we can. De deacons will spread de word dat we will haves a special prayer meeting 'morrow night. To pray for peace 'n' calm in our community. My message will be to turns de other cheek...but I needs yo word...I needs both yo words dat de sheff's department will do all yo can to calms down de white peoples...'specially all dem rebel rousers."

Rocky stood up and extended his hand, "You certainly have my word Brother Terrell."

"Yes sir," Spud added, "I promise you that the Sheriff's office will do everything in our power to tamp down tha troublemakers."

As Spud backed out of the preacher's driveway, he cleared his throat. "Rock...uh...you know that...uh under department protocol I'd be supposed to uh...you know, hold your badge and gun 'til...uh we get a ruling on tha shooting...uh."

Rocky nodded. "Hey man, it's okay. It's your job." He took his Glock out of the holster and unpinned his badge, then laid them both on the car's console between the two old friends.

NINETEEN

Associated Press Wire Service: Summer, Alabama 10:00 pm   *June 22, 1998*

Two mobile homes in the riot torn community of Westville have been destroyed by fire. Responding Summer fire department units were pelted with rocks and bottles and forced to leave the scene. Local sources are reporting that at least two firemen and one deputy sheriff sustained injuries from thrown objects. Summer County Chief Deputy, Spud Jordan, has ordered officers out of the community. Alabama Governor, Bog Allen, has declared a state of emergency in Westville and mobilized the Alabama National Guard to enforce a dusk to dawn curfew.

Mulberry Road   Summer County   11:30 pm   June 23, 1998

Ted rubbed his tired eyes. This was yet another endless and bumpy night patrol with Rocky. The deputy broke the extended quiet. "Do you like your boss back in Chicago?"

Ted lit a cigarette. "Yes I do. Like *and* respect. My editor is the most solid person I've ever known."

"Hmm, I've noticed you don't really respect many people. He must be a helluva guy."

"My boss is a woman. She's smart, tough and cool under fire, but she also has genuine compassion...and the kind of moral compass you don't find much in this world.

153

If Susan Rollins told me to cover a story on the backside of Hell, I'd buy a ticket and pack my bags."

Rocky drove on silent again for a full minute. "You know, what you just said about her, that's *exactly* the way I've always felt about J.P. I've always said if I had to be in a foxhole with somebody, J.P. would be the guy I'd choose."

"Yeah well, in my foxhole, the "guy" would be Susan."

After a long stretch of potholes and silence, Ted turned toward Rocky. "Nobody in the police establishment seems to be making any effort to find out who, other than Malachi, might have molested Callie Baines. What about rounding up the usual local suspects? Surely even Summer has some registered sex offenders."

"No, really very few, registered or non-registered. There *is* one strange dude that's always been suspicious, but I can tell you that he's gonna be a total waste of time."

Ted pulled out his pocket notebook and tiny flashlight. "Who are you talking about and why is he a waste of time?"

Rocky sighed, "Well his name is Dexter Lee Grayson. He's about 40. Lived here off and on with his silver spoon since he was born. He's gotta bleached pony-tail, gold earrings and alligator boots kinda look. He travels with this weird doctor all over the world. People have always said that both of them are bi-sexual and both of them have a taste for kids – girls and boys."

Ted stopped scribbling under his dim penlight. "Wow. That doesn't sound like your typical Southern Baptist resident! So why would a hard look at him be a waste of time?"

"Okay...number one, Dexter and Doctor Strange Glove always go to Asia or someplace in the spring for three or four months. I think they went to Thailand back in April. Number two, his aunt will always cover his tracks and she's got more land and money than God! Not to mention every politician on the planet in her back pocket! And number three, the sheriff's department has looked into Dexter and the doctor, Colvin Dupree, several times before. Nothing ever turns up. Heck, Dexter even passed a school board background check to teach a high school art class!"

Ted looked up from his notebook. "But I can tell you *think* he's doing something wrong with kids."

Rocky hit a bone-jarring hole. "Umph! Well, thinking and *proving* are two different things. I've always heard that they like to go to Bangkok and these places where you can buy young kids like a sack of groceries. But here in Summer, all we've ever had to go on was coffee shop gossip. No child or anyone else has ever made an official complaint. Not that it would matter much. Anna Grayson, with all her clout, would probably save his sorry fat ass anyway."

"So I assume Anna Grayson is Dexter Lee Grayson's aunt? Does she live here in Summer?"

Rocky laughed sarcastically. "The Grayson's live any damn place they want. Anna chooses to live here because she still owns most of the town!"

"So where did she get all her money?"

"Her grandfather was Colonel Jacob Grayson. In the early 1900's he bought hundreds of thousands of acres in Alabama and founded Grayson Timber Company. I think as recent as the 1960's, the Grayson's were still the largest private land holders in

155

the state...maybe in the Southeast. Anna's old man, Harley, pissed away a lot of it, but she's still loaded."

Ted closed his notebook, "Is she approachable? You think she would give me an interview?"

Rocky chuckled then broke into a long hearty laugh. "You could probably get an interview because you're a well-known big shot writer...but," he laughed again, "when she realizes you are trying to dig up some dirt on Dexter, she will absolutely chew you up and spit you out!"

"So you're warning me that Anna Grayson is a hand-full?"

Rocky smiled and shook his head in the dark patrol car. "You're gonna have to see for yourself. Let's just say she's colorful when she's sober and *extremely* colorful when she's not!"

Summer, Alabama   *10:00 am*   *June 24, 1998*

Ted paused at the black wrought iron gate and glanced over his shoulder at the imposing Summer courthouse just two blocks away. He turned back toward the two-story Victorian house and walked up the shady slate sidewalk. He immediately heard birds singing high above his head in the leafy branches of the enormous oaks that lined the front walk. As he climbed the front steps a warm breeze washed his face with the luscious smell of blooming flowers. He pushed the lighted button and heard a pleasant rhythmic bell chime inside followed shortly by steady footsteps approaching the door.

A tall black man wearing a pressed white shirt and blue bowtie opened the door and looked him in the eye. "Good morning sir. I assume you are Mr. Logan, here to see Miss Grayson." Ted fumbled in his pants pocket and pulled out his press card. The man glanced at the ID with an amused half smile. "Yes Mr. Logan. She is waiting for you in the back parlor. Please follow me."

His polished mannerisms are well practiced and his English is perfect. I'll bet the old gal picked out his clothes.

The shiny hardwood creaked under their steps as they passed through a long foyer lined with assorted paintings in elaborate frames. They stepped into a spacious room filled with antique furniture that featured an all glass back wall that looked out over a back yard patio. Anna Grayson was seated on a crimson velvet sofa facing the patio with her back to the men. "Mr. Logan to see you, Miss Grayson."

Without turning her head she replied in a raspy voice, "Thank you James."

She made a faint gesture with her right arm above the back of the sofa. "Come around and have a seat."

Ted walked into the sunny room and paused in front of a Queen Anne chair positioned at a right angle to the seated woman. "Hello Miss Grayson. I'm Ted Logan with Newslink."

She turned her head and looked at him for the first time. She was wearing a lemon yellow low-cut summer dress and seated in a relaxed semi-slumped posture.

Much younger looking and more petite than Rocky had made her sound. He shifted his weight and extended his hand.

"Oh just have a seat. I know *who* you are. What I'd like to know is why in hell you're standing in *my* parlor!"

He settled into the ornate chair and studied the small blonde woman. "Okay, well I appreciate you taking the time to see me."

He saw a twinkle form in her soft blue eyes looking over a pair of tiny half-lens glasses. "Oh gads! I've always got time for a man with some breeding."

She's already got me off balance.

He cleared his throat, "Well, I am definitely *not* well-bred, but I would like to talk to you about the recent events in your town."

She caught Ted's brief glance at her prominent cleavage. "Yes honey, the twins *are* pretty damn firm for a chick my age!" She gave him a coy wink and spoke in a low animal like growl, "This fabulous face may have had a little tuck but the boobies are as natural as sin."

Damn it, could I please have a restart!

He pretended to ignore her comment and struggled to get back on track. "I understand that your family has a long history in Summer County."

She vigorously shook her head in disapproval. "You act as nervous as a long-tailed cat in a room full of rockers. Let's have some tea. James! James! Please bring in a pot." She gestured toward a row of portraits hanging on the oak paneled wall to her left. "Darling *my* family has a long history in the civilized world!"

Ted stood and walked toward the family gallery. He pointed at what looked like George Washington on a horse ready to ford the Potomac. "I'm guessing that's *not* the first president."

158

"No, but you're close. That *is* William Wesley Grayson, the first president's Chief of Staff."

He stepped closer and read the inscription under a smallish man in a World War I era uniform loaded with medals. "And this is your grandfather, Colonel Jacob Grayson?"

"Yes, of course. He could have gone right to the top of the army brass, but decided instead to buy every pine tree in the Western hemisphere."

The portrait to the Colonel's right was a man decked out in full papal regalia. "Wow! Is that the Pope?"

"Oh gads! No, No, No! That's my third cousin Rowan Collins, the Arch Bishop of Canterbury."

"So I guess the Grayson's are Episcopalian?"

"Oh honey yes! We are Anglican to the bottom of our precious little hearts."

The butler delivered a china tea service on a sterling silver tray and set it atop a small table beside Anna's sofa. "Would you like me to pour Miss Anna?"

"No James, that's all." The coy look returned to her face as she opened a small drawer under the table and produced a pewter flask. "Mr. Logan, would you like a little sweetener in your tea?"

"Just call me Ted, and no thanks. I'll just take the plain tea."

She opened the flask and filled one cup almost to the brim with the "sweetener" before pouring the steaming brown liquid into Ted's cup and topping her own cup with just a splash from the pot.

He took the hot cup from her and struggled to get a long finger inside the dainty handle. He sat back down and took a careful sip. "May I call you Anna?"

"Of course darling. I'd be offended if you didn't."

"So Anna, you and your nephew are the only Graysons who still live in Summer?"

"Oh gads, Dexter Lee stores his luggage in my guest house out back but he *lives* all over the globe!" She seemed to be suddenly focused on the back lawn.

Ted twisted and followed her intense stare out through the open sliding glass doors onto the lush manicured grounds around a stone patio. *Looks like the 16th green at Augusta National. What does she see?*

Anna reached behind the tea table and in one fluid motion pulled out and pointed a double barrel shotgun.

At the shattering concussion of the blast, Ted jumped straight up out of his chair spilling hot tea onto his lap. "My God Anna!"

She calmly returned the smoking gun to its rack behind the table. "I hate those damn chipmunks, but that's one more little bastard blown to hell!" She picked up her tea cup and smiled serenely at Ted. "Oh dear I hope you didn't burn the family jewels. Should I have James bring you a towel?"

He sat back down and hoped his voice didn't sound as rattled as he felt. "No, I'm okay." *What a bizarre morning after a bizarre month of following a bizarre trail!*

She emptied her cup in quick little gulps. The pungent smell of gun smoke hung heavy in the room. "So *Ted*, I've been reading your articles. All the democrats over in Westville are burning down their own nests. You and Paul Harvey are talking to Malachi Baines – who's as crazy as a road lizard – and Billy Bob Clinton's pulled his cigar out of Monica's twat long enough to order his Fed's on a death march. You've written your squalid little stories – so why are you talking to me?" She refilled her cup from the flask. "You want more tea?"

"No thanks for the tea. I'm here because I think you know the local people better than most. I still don't know much about the allegations made by the Baines' daughter – which are what started this whole episode in the first place."

Her head wobbled slightly as she gulped more tea. "What in the name of grandma's bible makes you think I know anything about the little hillbilly urchin?"

Ted's ears were ringing from the shotgun blast and the wet, throbbing blister on his right thigh was really hurting. "Well, I'm trying to talk to anybody in town or from Summer High School who had any contact with Callie Baines. I know that Dexter Grayson taught an art class at the school. Since Dexter's not available, I decided to ask you if Dexter knows Callie Baines."

She emptied her tea cup again. "Dexter Lee hardly has *contact* with anyone in Summer except the good doctor Colvin." Her eyes were beginning to glaze over. She retrieved the flask and to Ted's amazement openly popped some pills in her mouth and washed them down from the "sweetener" container. "Dexter...Dexter brings those...those school brats over for...for art lessons out of...out of pure boredom darrrling." She slumped deeper on the sofa and got still.

James immediately entered the room and looked at Anna. "Mr. Logan I think you better come back another time."

Ted stood up and was briskly escorted down the front hall. The butler hesitated with his hand on the massive door handle. "Mr. Logan...uhh," he shook his head and looked down at the floor, "Good day, Mr. Logan."

Bug Peppers had just poured Ted's second Jack on the rocks when Rocky joined him at one of the grill's wobbly tables. "So you had tea today with Queen Anna?"

"Yeah, and that was the damndest interview I've had in 30 years. You're not gonna believe what she did! She..."

Rocky interrupted, "She probably shot a chipmunk out the living room window."

"Hell yes! How did you know? I'm still deaf in both ears!"

Rocky smiled, "Oh yeah. She's done that many times before. I'm surprised there's still a live chipmunk left in her yard."

Ted raised his arms and rubbed both ears. "She's outrageous! She got looped on 'tea' and pills. Passed out cold before I left. What the heck does she take?"

"I suspect Anna and Dexter get any drug they want any time they want it. The Grayson's have always used their private doctors like street corner pimps." Rocky leaned back and propped his muddy boots on the seat of an empty chair. "When I was a kid I heard stories about Anna's parents. On practically a monthly basis, they would arrange private ambulance trips over to the Westshire Clinic in Atlanta."

"Sounds like a pair of spoiled hypochondriacs."

"Oh it was that and more. Her old man did claim he had over 50 surgeries! They both stayed high on medical prescriptions most of their adult lives. Supposedly, Harley Grayson's estate left the Westshire Clinic five million dollars."

Ted stopped rubbing his ringing ears. "Anna is more attractive than I expected. How old is she?"

Rocky wrinkled his brow, "Oh I guess she's probably late 60's. She oughta look good! I'm sure she's had the best re-building job money can buy."

"Yeah well, she made it clear that at least one notable part of her anatomy is still original equipment!"

"Damn! Are there no limits to what a Chicago reporter will ask a Southern lady?"

"Just doing my job. I assume she's been married at some point."

"Oh she's been married at *every* point. This is probably just a temporary lull to give her lawyers time to tweek the next prenuptial agreement. Parnell Gilbert was the most recent. I think he was number five or six. Rumor is, Parnell has been institutionalized with some sort of mental breakdown."

Ted nodded his head. "Yeah I can feel his pain. So Anna never had any kids?"

"No, none of her own. She and the hired help did raise Dexter. He is her sister Margaret's son. For years the whole crew – Margaret, Dexter, Anna and assorted husbands lived out on the family plantation. They call it Lee Hall. I've never heard anything about Dexter's father. He's always used his mother's last name. She died of an overdose when Dexter was six or seven."

Ted leaned toward Rocky. "I think you need to find out if Callie Baines was one of Dexter Grayson's high school art students. Anna seemed to say that Dexter would bring the students to his place for private lessons. Would the high school allow that?"

Rocky put his feet on the floor and set up straight. "Okay, I will find out. But I don't believe Malachi or Becky would approve of Callie taking art classes. Home-ec maybe, but not art. And I don't know about any high school students going over there for lessons. Now, people *do* take lessons at Dexter's place. Skeeter's sister, Marlene, took lessons over there for a while last year. There's supposed to be an art gallery behind the guest house in the old horse barn."

TWENTY

Ted leaned against the knotty rail of the cabin's tiny front porch and slowly exhaled a gusher of cigarette smoke. In the cool summer darkness, he could faintly hear dogs barking across the lake. He twisted around on his rough support and turned his good ear toward the distant sounds. *Were they farm dogs barking at a raccoon or a wild pack moving in for the kill? According to Rocky, east across the lake was national forest land with very few inhabitants…beloved family pets or savage animals without inhibitions to kill a human?* As Ted pondered the possibilities, a cold chill ran up the back of his neck.

When the cell phone rang in his pocket, he jumped straight up. "Shit! What the hell time is it?...Hello!"

"Ted, this is Ben Golden"

"Damn it Golden, it's 3:30 in Baltimore. Don't you sleep at night?"

"Actually, we work primarily at night and you did say to call the minute I completed the work-up"

"So I guess you have something on my favorite sheriff?"

"Yes, I do think we have mined all there is to retrieve from Mr. Jordan's financial records. I don't know what you're looking for but here is a quick summary. J.P. Jordan and his wife have no regular income other than two salaries. They have received proceeds from two timber sales in the last five years from a 300 acre tract of land they own jointly with a Robert Dees. Each sale netted them just under $15,000. They own their home, two automobiles, a $3000 savings account and have less than $200 in a joint checking account. They have no recorded debt of any kind."

"Not much out of the ordinary so far," Ted interrupted.

"Well, yes and no," Gold continued, "It is unusual at their age with no debt to service, that they have not accumulated any significant savings."

"Do you think they have money hidden somewhere?"

"No Ted, I do not. By analyzing their expenditures, I can account for 99% of their income for the past decade."

"Anything unusual about how they spend their money?"

"Well…there are two noteworthy patterns. J.P. Jordan has always written 100% of the checks from their joint accounts, and for at least ten years, he has written a large check on the 25th of each month to the same person. This one payment really stands out because it is now $5000 and represents 60% of their total monthly income. As a result, the average month end balance in their account has been declining in recent years. They closed out May with $150.00 in their bank account."

"Damn! That is interesting. Who is the check written to?"

"The checks are made payable to G.L. Spook and mailed to a post office box in Atlanta. The checks are then endorsed by Spook and converted to cash at an Atlanta bank."

"Who the hell is G.L. Spook? Any leads on their identity?"

"No. We have checked all databases in the state of Georgia for last name Spook and first names starting with a G and second names with an L. There are none. The paper trail to G.L. Spook ends at PO Box 9385 Atlanta, Georgia."

Dye's Landing, Summer County   *9:35 am*   *June 25, 1998*

Ted squinted to see the tiny cell phone digits and dialed Cher Lavoe's number at the New York News from memory. "Hello Babe."

"Teddy! What a nice surprise. I wish I could believe this means you are missing me terribly, but since it is now almost July and the last time *you called me* was maybe April, I'm thinking you must need a whopping big favor!"

"Well…ah…yeah, but I really have missed you."

She laughed, "Oh Teddy, you're so cute when you get busted!"

He chuckled. Hearing her voice still made him feel warm and mushy. "Well babe, you've nailed me again. I do sorta need your help."

"Mmmm. I see. If you *sorta need my help*, I'm guessing you've stepped into a southern fried rat's nest down there."

"Yeah, I guess you *could* say that. Look babe, I was wondering if you could fly into Atlanta for a few days of checking around and maybe get that FBI agent you know there to trace down a P.O. box owner."

She laughed again. "Oh this is good! Let me get it straight. You want me to leave *my* job for several days to work for *you* AND you want me to arrange a felony ID theft from a Federal Post Office by working with special agent Jim Taylor…who as you know, will do anything I ask as long as I promise him my body. Am I missing anything here?"

"Ah…well I guess that's sorta the bottom line…as long as you *promise* Taylor everything and give him nothing!"

"Uh huh, that's easy for you to say Mr. Logan! Have you ever had a G-man's eyes lust after every step you take?"

"No. The agents I work with just lust after my superior knowledge!"

She sighed, "Teddy you already know I'm going to do this for you. Do I ever tell you 'no' about anything?"

"No babe, you don't and I sure as hell don't know why. But you know I'd do the same for you and I really *have* missed seeing you."

"Well this is going to cost you big boy. You better plan on packing your bags for New York the day you put this story to bed! And I don't mean for an overnight trip…at least a week, maybe two weeks this time."

He laughed, "I was going to do that anyway. I promise. Two full weeks. Broadway plays. The whole nine yards."

"Okay. Don't you dare lie to me about it!" Her tone changed. She was now the consummate professional. "Give me the P.O. Box and zip code along with who you think we are looking for and why."

Ted brought Cher up to date on his investigation and the mysterious $5000 payments J.P. Jordan regularly mailed to G.L. Spook. She agreed to be in Atlanta the following morning.

"Oh babe, one more thing. Since I've been down here I've done a lot of thinking…Lots of time on my hands in the backwoods…And ah, I think you and I should talk again when I'm in New York…Really talk again. Life is short babe…So damn short."

Wayford, Alabama   *12:00 noon*   *June 25, 1998*

Rocky glanced again in his rear view mirror. "I wish J. Riley's lab geeks would keep up with me. They're gonna get lost yet." He rubbed his short hair. "I'm not sure I buy this dog DNA strategy. J. Riley says it could prove the dogs we killed in Junee Bottoms are direct descendants of the Grant's Brothers hog dogs. But even if you do, some people are still gonna say the wild dogs belong to Malachi."

Ted lit a cigarette. "I guess he's counting on a judge believing the dog's lineage supports the theory of the Grants turning dogs loose in the forest."

"I hope he gets his money's worth. I hear this test is going to cost him 20 grand."

Ted thumped ashes out a small crack in his passenger side window. "Look, there's something I need to tell you. I've found a source that knows J.P. Jordan has mailed a $5000 check to somebody in Atlanta every month for at least 10 years. This monthly payment is the reason he's out of money. The night poachers you nailed were right. Jordan's in a serious financial crunch."

Rocky clenched his jaw and drove silently for several miles before responding. "I don't feel right about you digging into J.P.'s private business…but if he's in some kind of trouble, maybe he needs my help. What have you found out?"

"Not much, except he mails the check every month to a G.L. Spook. Does that name ring a bell?"

"Nope, I don't know of any Spooks. How you gonna find out who it is?"

"My ex-wife, Cher Lavoe, is flying to Atlanta to trace down G.L. Spook."

"Your ex-wife?"

"Yeah, she's an absolute top notch investigative reporter with tons of awards to prove it."

"So, is she with Newslink?"

"No, we worked together at Newslink in the 1980's. She started out as my intern. She's been with the New York News since 1989."

"And your *ex-wife* is willing to drop what she's doing in New York and fly down here to help you? That doesn't sound like any ex I've ever heard of. Do all your ex's line up to do your dirty work?"

"Not *exactly*. This one's very different. She's special. We're still pretty close."

"Damn! She sounds way too special to be just an ex! Do you still love her?" Rocky stared at Ted. "Will you always love her?"

Ted sucked in hard on his cigarette. "Helluva question for *you* to be asking. Do you still love Skeeter? Will you always love her?"

"We're not talking about me."

"Well I'm talking about you now. I believe you should jump at the chance to marry Skeeter Yates."

Rocky grinned. "And I believe you would jump at the chance to sleep with Skeeter Yates."

Ted bit down hard on his cigarette butt. "Is it that damn obvious?"

Rocky glanced at Ted. "It doesn't bother me. I wouldn't think your blood was red if she didn't flip your switches."

Ted crushed out his smoke. "Let's make a pact and agree not to talk about any woman we're not watching on a video."

"You got it!"

In a few more minutes they turned up the chert driveway to Hammer Grant's house with the lab guys' white van on their bumper. There were rusting vehicles scattered though knee-high grass in every direction around the unpainted rambling house. When their SUV crunched to a stop, Ted could hear dogs barking from both sides of the Tahoe and strangely, a rooster crowing. When Ted stepped out, his foot crushed an empty beer can. A small wiry man with greasy shoulder length hair immediately confronted Rocky talking 90 miles an hour.

"Now look here now Barnett, we ain't broke no law. We ain't wanting no trouble. I done told you to test my dogs. I ain't never turned no dogs loose on purpose nowhere. I done told that lawyer man what I'm telling you. He promised me they'd be

171

no trouble with the law for me 'n' Joe. Maybe we might get a little money to testify and for our trouble and all."

When he paused to catch his breath, Rocky interjected, "Okay Hammer, just slow down. We are here to take a saliva sample from a few dogs. Snap a few pictures. I just need you to keep your catch dogs from taking these guys' arms off."

"Yeah sure. All my bitin' dogs is tied up right now. Jest come on around this way." The faded overall-clad dog owner limped toward the sagging back corner of the ancient farm house. A few steps up the driveway a large black dog lurched at Ted with a growling bark. When he reached the end of his heavy chain, he fought against the restraint and grabbed the chain in his frothing mouth.

Ted quickly stepped toward Rocky. "What a nice pooch. Who collects his DNA?"

Behind the house, near a ramshackled gray barn, were several dozen dogs and pups. Most of the grown dogs were staked to a chain with a metal barrel for shelter. Several were contained in a wood-tin-wire patchwork pen adjacent to the weathered barn with a battered Volkswagen body serving as a community dog house. Two groups of puppies were housed in what appeared to be old chicken coops. The dogs were mostly black or reddish in color with large bodies. At all ages, they had oversized bull dog shaped heads. The whole kennel area had the pervasive rank odor of excrement and the numbing sounds of constant aggressive barks and growls.

Joe Grant was waiting at the dog pens. He was a clone of his brother with more tattoos and fewer teeth. "I was just ah thinking 'bout what you fellas is trying to do here.

Now we ain't never left no dogs up there on purpose, but some of them dogs we tried out never would let us catch 'em and some of our ole bitch dogs we still got here."

Rocky pointed toward the Volkswagen pen. "I see several older females. Are you saying they might be old enough to have whelped some of the dogs you *lost* up in the national forest?"

Joe spit tobacco juice onto the foul mud. "Oh yeah, ole White Face there is 'bout twelve an Blackie's eight or nine. They both been squeezing out pups twice ah year since they was one. Neither one of 'em hardly got any insides back there, they done been nailed by studs so much."

Rocky gestured toward the lab technicians. "Okay, these guys need to push a cotton swab inside each dog's mouth. So get the two oldest bitches out of the pen and hold them tight so nobody looses any fingers."

"Shaa. We'll jest drag 'em in tha barn and strap 'em in tha breeding harness. They's use to that. Bitches can't even move their heads. Then you can stick anything you want in either end of 'em."

Summer, Alabama   *7:30 pm*   *June 25, 1998*

Leap frogging each other around the green carpet of freshly mowed lawn, the two young rabbits frolicked in the growing shadows of late afternoon. J.P. Jordan propped his sock feet on the cedar deck railing and watched the cottontails play in his quiet back yard. The annoying rattle of the patio door signaled Marabell was coming to join him. She shoved the door open, then tripped over the threshold. "Oh gosh sugar, that door almost got me!" She stumbled up against him and slapped at a yellow fly buzzing near his beefy neck. "You're all hot under your bandages sugarplum and these darn bugs are eating you alive! I'm gonna get you a big ole glass of iced tea and a flyswatter."

In a few minutes, she waddled back out with a tall green glass in one hand and a screen-wire fly flap in the other. J.P. sipped his tea and continued to gaze quietly at the now stationary rabbits. "What's on your mind sugar? I can tell it's something big. I guess after all these tragic deaths and now the National Guard marching around with machine guns over at Westville...," she shook her head. "Now you've been shot. It's almost too much for any mortal man to handle."

J.P. sat his tea glass on the floor and winced with pain. "You're right Bellie. It would be almost too much anyway, but..." his husky voice broke, "when it's all your own fault...it is too much. Just too much."

She lunged and hugged his broad torso from behind. "No! No! No! J.P. Jordan this is not your fault! None of this! That wicked man Baines, those stubborn agents that wouldn't listen to you, those hot-headed black boys in Westville. *They* are all responsible...but not you!"

J.P. wiped his eyes. "It all started with me. My bad decisions – and now it's brought something back from a long time ago. J. Riley Summer wants to finish what his old man started and do me in. That's the real reason he's over here helping Malachi Baines."

"Oh pooh! Old John Summer was just plain jealous. Jealous that you were elected sheriff so young. He used to say you only got it because of your daddy being sheriff. *That's* why he tried to make trouble for you back then. You put that old worm in

174

his place then and you're going to do the same with Junior now!" She squeezed her plump figure between his chair and the rail and got right in his face. "You listen to me J.P. Jordan! You were elected sheriff because you were just as qualified as your daddy. To this day, you are the best sheriff Summer has ever had. You are better than any of these uppity-up Summers and I'm going to make sure you prove it one more time!"

He looked away from her. "No, Bellie, I was not the man my father was back then and I'm sure as hell not today. John Summer knew what you could never see."

Associated Press Wire Service: Birmingham, AL *June 26, 1998*

U.S. Attorney, Alice Morgan, announced a federal grand jury has indicted Malachi Baines in the June 14 murders of five federal agents near Tate's Gap Alabama. Sources familiar with the proceedings told the A.P. that F.B.I. investigators discovered a man-made cave on the north bank site of the Coon Creek bridge disaster. Engineers testified that the cavern was dug five feet below the north bridge abutment and designed to be flooded with water in order to compromise the stability of the bridge supports. Prosecutors argued that only Baines had the means and the motive to flood the cave and thus trigger the collapse that lead to the 5 deaths. A federal arrest warrant on 5 counts of first degree murder is expected later today. On June 18, the 11th Circuit Court of Appeals dismissed a weapons charge indictment brought against Baines, however federal and state murder charges for the dog mauling deaths of three sheriff's deputies are still pending.

Summer, Alabama *1:00 pm* *June 28, 1998*

Seated in his rental car, Ted rapidly scribbled notes on a yellow legal pad. His observations and thoughts from yet another high profile event in Summer County were rapidly being assimilated for Monday's Newslink headliner. "Fanning the Flames of Tragedy." It read, "Sunday morning the reverend Thurgood Johnson led a small army of

175

civil rights protestors into Summer, Alabama. Rev. Johnson and Los Angeles attorney, Lucius Cockrell, spoke to worshippers at Westville A.M.E. Church and later led a 1960's style protest march two miles from the Harlan B. Summer Bridge to the Alabama National Guard barricade on the outskirts of Westville. Johnson and Cockrell contend that the May 19th shooting death of black deputy sheriff, Willie Gaddis, was racially motivated on the part of indicted deputy Buck Yancey and the Summer County Sheriff's Department. The marchers, escorted by state troopers and sheriff's deputies, were prevented from entering the town of Westville by riot gear equipped guardsman. Today's march, marred by rock throwing incidents and at least a dozen shouting matches with irate white groups, culminates weeks of racial violence in this small rural county."

Ted recounted the numerous racial encounters that had resulted in deaths or injuries since May 19th and the incendiary rhetoric espoused over that time by Cockrell, Johnson and other outside figures. He concluded with, "The indictment of Buck Yancey notwithstanding, the exact nature of Willie Gaddis' death remains cloudy. There is no credible evidence to support the theory of a larger conspiracy by the sheriff's office. In spite of these facts, national civil rights leaders have pounced on the opportunity to arouse local tensions for their own political or financial gains. Summer County has just over 20,000 residents, less than 4,000 of which are black. In the past two decades there has not been a single incident reported in the county as a racially motivated act of violence. Yet, on this bright June morning, 3,000 vocal out-of-state protestors, escorted by 200 state and local police officers, went head to head with 1,100 armed national guardsmen. An estimated 400 newsmen and reporters were on hand to cover the 'made for television' confrontation. The formerly quiet county is now a human powder keg on the brink of explosion. Will prominent activists from three time zones away fan the flames that forever implode a peaceful way of life?"

Rocky walked up the broad white steps and smiled at the pretty woman waiting for him in her front porch swing. "Hello Marlene."

"Rocky Barnett, come over here and sit down." She gestured toward the empty side of the swing. "I haven't seen you in a month of Sundays!"

"Yeah, I reckon it has been a while. That day I called you about Dexter Lee, I told Skeeter I don't think I've seen you since your mama's Easter dinner."

"Well that's right and my baby sister's not much better. She used to bowl with me and the girls every Thursday night but she's not showed up for several months. You tell that lil' Skeeter hussy big sis is gonna whoop her if she don't come around more!"

Rocky grinned. "Yeah, I think everybody's been all out of whack around here lately."

Marlene's smooth face scowled into worry lines and she stared out across the waves of blooming flowers in her manicured front lawn. "I know it's been so bad for everybody. Verna, Sally, Sue and Juanita all lost their husbands and then those Marshals too. Dave Ellis is disfigured for life…and Rocky, ain't this all because Callie Baines claims her daddy molested her?" She placed her hand gently on Rocky's arm. "I know you don't believe Malachi did anything to Callie…and I really don't know anything for

177

sure either. But I called you 'cause I've been thinking for weeks 'bout something I saw a few months ago and I wanna tell you 'bout it."

He patted her hand. "Sure Marlene. I'm glad you feel like you can always talk to me."

"Well, you know every now and again I fill in for Bonnie Duke and drive that Tate's Gap school bus run. Callie's nearly always on that bus and she's tha last kid dropped off in the evening. Well around the first of May, I made tha afternoon run for Bonnie. I let Callie off 'bout 3:30 or so and then I pulled down to Tate's store to get a Coke and talk to Mavis and them. Callie always gets dropped off up tha road a little piece from the store right where the Baines road hits the Tate's Gap road. In bad weather, she waits for her momma in that old barn there at the intersection. As far as I know, Becky was the only one that *used* to pick her up. That day it was kinda dark and rainy. I stayed at tha store 'til nearly 4:30 – I know it was nearly 4:30 'cause they had the radio on "Tell it and Sell it" and it was just going off. I'd left the bus parked sorta catty-whompus in the store's lot and when I got back in, I noticed a truck stopped up around the curve at tha old barn. I thought about Callie and drove back by there real slow. Their ole red pick-up was out front of tha barn and I saw Malachi and Callie beside tha truck. I saw her jerk away from him. She was slapping at him and he was trying to push her in tha truck. I could tell she'd been crying. I don't know if that day means anything or not. Rocky, I just don't know."

TWENTY-ONE

Cher Lavoe slipped into a back corner booth at Pizza Plaza inside the Hartsfield terminal and pushed Ted's number on her speed dial. "I've got all the scoop Teddy and you *really, really* owe me! You had better be in New York next month. I've already bought our theater tickets!"

"Well babe, I knew you would dig it out, but tell me you're not wearing an FBI agent's engagement ring!"

"I'm not telling you any such thing! You will just have to wonder *exactly* what I did all weekend to get this info!"

"Okay, Okay, be brutal. So what's the story?"

"Your G.L. Spook is Gina Lambert, formerly Gina Lambert Spook, who was married to George D. Spook from 1965 to 1977. She is a 56 year old Atlanta realtor… and through amazingly adept research, I learned she is J.P. Jordan's 3rd cousin!"

"Damn! That *is* great work. So what about the $5000 payments? Does she…"

"Trust me!" Cher interrupted, "I *have* the whole story. Gina Lambert Spook has received a monthly payment from J.P. Jordan since 1967. The amount has gone up over the years. It's been $5000 since about '96. Every month, Gina cashes the check and delivers a $5000 cash payment to the Mountain View nursing home in Atlanta. And…the payment is for the care of Elizabeth Rankin who has been a patient at this rather exclusive facility since September 1st 1967."

Ted was stunned. "Holy Moly! Who is Elizabeth Rankin and why is she there?

Cher cleared her throat. "In all honesty, I had to work a lot harder on this part. I had to fake an identity and make a $5000 payment to the home's weekend administrator to learn about Elizabeth – by the way, you can tell Susan Rollins she owes me the five grand. Elizabeth Rankin is J.P. Jordan's niece. She is the daughter of his late sister, Mildred Jordan Rankin. It took six long hours of digging online through Alabama newspaper archives from the 1960's, but I learned that Mildred died of natural causes June 2nd 1967. Elizabeth was her only child. According to the Mountain View administrator and an account in the Birmingham Herald, Elizabeth nearly drowned on the 4th of July 1967 at Oak Mountain State Park. She was rescued by lifeguards, but suffered permanent brain damage. She was 14 at the time. Now, here is the sketchy part…there is some suggestion it may have been a suicide attempt. Her stomach was pumped and large quantities of sleeping pills were discovered."

"Oh man, what a story. How's her condition today?"

"Physically, she's almost normal. She feeds herself, she does group exercises, but she has not spoken a word in 31 years. Her mind seems to be a blank. She does not appear to have any memory. She does not even recognize her nurses from one day to the next. And you're right about J.P. Jordan's financial trouble. According to the administrator, Gina Lambert is worried that she cannot continue to make the monthly payments. If Lambert stops paying, Elizabeth Rankin's future is uncertain."

"This is one helluva good job babe…but it's nothing like what I expected you to find."

"Yes, I know Teddy. You were hoping for something outrageously sordid, but all I've discovered is that your sheriff has secretly sacrificed for 30 years to generously provide for his afflicted niece."

Dye's Landing, Summer County   *6:00 pm*   *June 29, 1998*

The screen door swung open with a raspy screech. Rocky handed Ted a cold beer. "Come on in and have a seat." Ted collapsed into one of the cracked leather recliners and popped open his Bud. "Man! That's some story your ex-wife dug up. I remember hearing as a kid about J.P.'s sister and niece. I thought they had both died about the same time. I think his sister had cancer. Everybody thought the daughter committed suicide right after her mom died."

Ted sipped his beer. "Don't you think it's strange that you didn't know about Elizabeth Rankin all these years?"

Rocky extended his left arm and rubbed his old dog's head. Bo's tail beat a slow cadence on the cool pine floor. "Yeah, it's real strange. I practically grew up in his house. I never thought J.P. kept any secrets from me. I guess he had a good reason. Maybe he just didn't want to take any credit for all he was doing for the girl."

"Do you know Gina Lambert?"

"No, I never heard of her, but J.P.'s got some Lambert cousins over in Pineville."

181

Ted tapped his beer can. "There's got to be some reason for J.P. wanting people to believe Elizabeth died in 1967. Concealing his payments to the nursing home through G.L. Spook – a major charade's been going on there for years."

Rocky rubbed his forehead. "I'm not going to worry about why J.P.'s been doing a good thing…I'm worried about something else. I hiked back up to Piney Bald today – that's gotten to be a pain-in-the-ass in itself. With all the reporters and even the Feds tailing my butt, I had to duck and twist to lose the posse. Then Malachi…he was different today. He got really pissed when I asked about the May fight with Callie at the old barn. He said Marlene was just like all the other townspeople – trying to frame him for hurting his daughter – but it's clear that Malachi now believes *somebody* has molested Callie.

"Well, that could explain why he seemed so agitated."

"Yeah, but what worries me is he thinks he knows *who*, but he won't tell me. He said I couldn't do anything about it now even if I had the man's name." Rocky shook his head. "Malachi has always trusted me before. I just don't know what's different now."

Summer, Alabama   *10:00 am*   *June 30, 1998*

As James walked him back to Anna's parlor, Ted could sense the middle-aged man had something on his mind. Today the glass sided room was as dark as the rainy day outside. Fresh cut flowers in two large vases filled the seating area with the aromatic scents of the backyard gardens. Anna was seated in exactly the same spot on her sofa beside the ornate tea table. Ted faced her and extended his hand, "Good morning Anna.

182

Thank you for seeing me again." He was careful to keep his eyes trained on her face but did notice her more conservative, but form fitting, high neck teal dress.

She took his hand for a brief second then replied in an icy tone, "Well *Ted*, since I don't have a clue why you were here last week, I'm doubly damn mystified why you're here looking me over again! But have a seat anyway."

He sank into the high-backed chair. "Thank you. I would really like to learn more about your family and their history in Summer County."

"Oh really? Is it to bolster your natural Yankee bias toward the southern aristocracy or just to pull my family skeletons out of their privileged closets?"

He looked over at the tea service already atop the mahogany table. "I think I would like some tea and *please* add a little sweetener!"

A warm twinkle replaced the cold glare in her blue eyes. "I've already started without you, but you strike me as a man who can catch up fast." She poured from her flask into a tea cup and topped it off with steaming tea.

When he took the cup and passed it under his nose he instantly recognized the rich familiar smell. "Anna we like the same brand of sweetener."

"Oh gads! Don't tell me you're a Jack Daniels guy! I had you pegged as the vodka type. Where in heavens did you learn to appreciate redneck Tennessee whiskey?"

He grinned. "In a redneck bar on the south side of Chicago I guess."

"Okay, I won't tell a soul you drink with rednecks in Chicago if you spread the word I only drink 100-year-old brandy in my tea!"

"It's a deal Anna. So okay, please tell me more about you and your family. I'm getting..."

She leaned toward him and interrupted, "I think you liked me better in the little shicky-poo yellow dress!"

He cleared his throat and continued, "I'm getting the idea that the Summer's and the Grayson's were definitely the foundation blocks of this town."

She set up straight and raised her eyebrows high above her half-glasses and wagged a finger at him. "The Summers! The Summers! Darling they were definitely the newcomers! Nobody ever heard of them until the Civil War! A hundred years before that *two* Graysons signed the Declaration of Independence! The old fart general got this damn little backwoods county renamed 75 years *after* Grayson Hall was built at Harvard!"

Ted smiled to himself. *When she's animated she's really very attractive and could pass for 45.*

"And, And! Robert Sims Grayson was a U.S. Senator from Alabama before the Summers ever built a chicken coop in this state!"

"Okay, I see that I stand corrected. So were you born in Summer County? Where did you go to school?"

She settled back onto the sofa and took a long sip of tea. A red flush was now visible on her smooth face. "Darling I was born in Atlanta, but I grew up at Lee Hall and Bay Manor. And yes honey, I was kicked out of all the finest Episcopal boarding schools!"

"I know Lee Hall is the family plantation just outside of town. Where is Bay Manor?"

Oh heavens, that's *always* been our summer place down on the coast at Point Clear." She leaned back against the sofa and looked away from Ted. He could see in her face she was somewhere far away. "Bay Manor was such a delight. When I was young we could caravan down there in May every year. All the help would go! Mamie and Hester and Lillie. Even old Dr. Jackson would stay the summer with us. We had a stable of fine horses. We had shrimp boils on the bay. I met my first husband, Herbert Walker, playing croquet at Bay Manor! I loved those wonderful summers. Dexter loved it too."

She looked back at Ted and for the first time he saw sadness in her pretty eyes.

"We were at Bay Manor when Margaret died. She was just 28. Little Dex was 6. I guess he's been mine every since." She was a little wobbly, but proceeded to carefully re-mix a cup of her concoction.

He spoke softly, "Did Dexter have a hard time after his mother's death?"

She smiled and perked up. "Oh gads! I think he did just fine! Lucinda helped me with him for the next 20 years. Did he have it bad? No, no, no. In the winter time at Lee Hall, Lucinda would sit on the toilet seat and warm it for Dexter before he pottied. Every time! He was 25 years old before he ever had to touch a cold toilet. She did everrry thing for him darling." She wrinkled her nose and whispered with obvious pride, "Lucinda was his first love! Around 12 or 13. That boy's always had everything he wanted!"

She was already too plastered to notice the shock in Ted's voice. "Well...ah so I guess Dexter really wants to teach his art classes out back in his gallery. Do you know if he gave Callie Baines lessons out there?"

She fumbled and shook some pills out of a prescription bottle she pulled from the tea table drawer. When she washed them down, Ted knew he only had minutes left.

"That girl...that girl might...might have...have been back in...back in the barn. But who...who the hell cares about her! What about...what about me! Damn it! I've always...always been...poor little Anna...poor little rich girl Anna!" She struggled to her feet and staggered right up in Ted's face. "You...son of a bitch...you...you have no fricking idea! I am adopted! Damn it to hell...do you...do you hear me? I'm frigging adopted! I'm no more a friggin' Grayson than you...you son of a..."

James raced into the room and grabbed her around the waist from behind as she collapsed in a limp heap on top of the still seated reporter. "Maggie! Maggie! Come help me!" A thin young maid scooted in and helped James carry Anna out of the parlor through a door under the family portraits.

Ted let himself out the front door and sat down on the top porch step. He dug a Camel out and quickly lit up. *Damn! Just when I thought an Anna Grayson interview could not possibly get any more bizarre, it just did.*

He heard the massive door open and turned to see the butler step out. James sat down beside him. "Mr. Logan could I bum a smoke?"

Ted thumped him out a cigarette and handed him his match book. "Just call me Ted."

The butler lit up and blew out a cloud of smoke. "My name is not really James. I'm J Bo Dawkins. She decided years ago that J Bo did not sound like a proper English name." He smiled. "Believe it or not, I'm really a musician. I've got a little jazz band.

We've even recorded a few records. Obviously, I'm a *starving* musician. That's why I do what I do here all day."

"Well J Bo, after what I've seen in my two visits, you must be one heck of a strong guy to work for Anna Grayson."

He smiled. "You can get used to anything. I just do what I have to do. I know you don't see this, but Anna is really not a bad person. She's got a lot of issues. She's spoiled rotten and has a lot of strong opinions I don't share, but she's really not evil.

Ted looked at him. "What's your opinion of Dexter Grayson?"

He shook his head. "Anna at least has a conscience. Dexter is dead cold on the inside. He has no shame." J Bo tilted his head and blew a gusher of smoke straight up toward the sky-blue porch ceiling. "I'm pretty sure Dexter and Colvin have sex with under-age kids on a regular basis. I've never actually seen it happen, but I know about something that might prove it."

"What is that J Bo?"

"They keep trophies – underwear, panties and boxer shorts. I don't know who it all belonged to. I don't know whether it's from kids or grown-ups, but I do know exactly where it's all locked up. I have occasion to go back there when Anna sends me. In the art gallery on the bottom floor of the old barn – they have a wall safe – that's where they keep it. I watched through the window one day when Dexter was playing with his collection."

"Damn! That could be a huge cache of evidence...would you recognize Callie Baines? Do you know if she took lessons from Dexter in the barn?"

"Yeah I know who she is. Her mother's picked her up here lots of times in that red pick-up. Anna hated it because that old Ford always leaked oil on her cobblestone driveway."

Ted slammed the car door and walked briskly up Rocky's front steps. He burst through the door without knocking. Bo raised his grey head off the floor and let out a muted bark.

"My old dog's gonna bite your butt if you don't start knocking first!"

Ted stepped over the big Lab. "You're not gonna believe what I just learned."

Rocky twisted around in his recliner and raised his hand like a traffic cop at an intersection. "Whoa...hold on. Let me go first." He reached to the floor and held up a manila folder. "You made a good call. It's all right here in these Summer High School documents. Callie *was* in Dexter Grayson's art classes the past two semesters and she *did* get private tutoring at Dexter's gallery over the last 10 months. Her mother signed more than 30 individual permission slips for the after-school lessons. But I'll still bet you Malachi didn't know Becky was letting her go."

Ted sighed and sat down in the empty rocker beside Rocky. "I've already confirmed that Callie was taking lessons at Dexter's gallery."

"Well I'll bet my ass that Anna didn't stay conscious long enough to confirm that!"

"Actually she did, but more importantly James – J Bo verified it and raised the possibility that an undergarment belonging to Callie *may be* locked up in the barn as a trophy! Can't you get a warrant to search the place now?"

"No I can't. Without Callie making a specific allegation, it's a hear-say fishing expedition at best. Anna's lawyers would blow that up in a heartbeat! You still don't get the clout she has. All you've seen is a half-stoned wild woman. She has another side. The local paper reported the various Grayson trusts just gave $250,000 to the Governor's re-election campaign and another $100,000 to the Attorney General. When Anna Grayson is sober, she is a shrewd power player."

Ted threw up his hands. "So what do you suggest? That you just do nothing with what is possibly irrefutable DNA evidence?"

Rocky rubbed his forehead. "I don't know man. I will take this to J.P. He has a lot of goodwill and clout of his own with the powers that be. I know at this point he would do anything in his power to bring this whole mess to an end. If he buys into what we've found, he might see a way to squeeze a warrant around the Grayson road blocks." Rocky dropped the folder back onto the worn pine floor. "And I did call Skeeter's sister Marlene to ask about her art lessons in Dexter's barn. She didn't see anything going on back there...but there is a strange painting hanging on the wall that Callie Baines signed. Marlene said it looked like a big ugly spider that had grown a pretty set of butterfly wings."

TWENTY-TWO

A hyped and highly anticipated Harry Prince Live show was rolling live to 15 million American viewers. Harry's guest for the entire show was J. Riley Summer. Prince led off with "Malachi Baines is facing a veritable plethora of federal and state criminal charges. The basis for many of these charges involves the theory that Baines owned and trained the 'guard' dogs that killed three deputy sheriffs. Counselor, I understand that tonight you intend to dispute this assertion by producing some incredible new *DNA evidence*? Tell us about this."

Summer launched into a very convincing explanation of the new DNA technology and the indisputable proof that two of the killer dogs were whelped by a female still owned by Joe and Hammer Grant in Wayford Alabama. All of the dogs killed in the attack were descendents of animals in the Grant's kennel. He went on to say that he had collected sworn affidavits from the Grant bothers and five other people establishing that Grant dogs had escaped from hunting excursions in the Cherokee National Forest between 1985 and 1993.

Prince seemed impressed, but still skeptical. "But Counselor, what's to say that the Baines family did not re-capture these feral beasts and train them for their own use?"

J. Riley smiled and produced the first of several visual aides prepared for the show. "Harry this is an aerial photograph shot from a helicopter 300 feet above the Baines farm. These are photos from every sector of this small homestead. There is simply no evidence of any capacity to kennel, hold or transport animals of this size and temperament."

Prince persisted, "But what if Malachi Baines had accomplices? Aren't there other Baines family members living in that area? Couldn't someone else have kenneled and transported those killer dogs?"

"Actually Harry, the answers are 'no' and 'no'. The site where the deputies were killed is over a linear mile from the Malachi Baines home but nearly six miles to the next closest residence. The deputies staged their ill-fated raid from the only road within 10 square miles. No resident within twenty-five square miles owns dogs similar to the killer animals nor has the means to contain or transport them. Harry, there is no possible way that Malachi Baines or anyone else could have owned, trained or controlled these feral animals." J. Riley's smooth voice took a more dramatic pitch, "The Summer County Sheriff knows this, the Alabama Attorney General knows this, and the U.S. Attorney knows this. Forty-one days after the attack, Malachi Baines has yet to be indicted on the dog mauling for a very basic reason. There is simply not one ounce of proof to establish his culpability!"

Harry Prince nodded somberly. "Well, you certainly make a convincing argument on the dogs, but Baines *has* in fact been indicted on other murder charges. How do you respond to the evidence that he sabotaged the bridge and caused the deaths of five federal agents?"

J. Riley Summer did not flinch. "I *respond* Harry, with solid facts." Summer began to methodically narrate a series of high definition photographs displayed for the viewers. "Allegedly a tunnel was built and flooded by Malachi Baines to collapse the bridge. This frame is a close-up of the walls and ceiling of the tunnel in question. Geologists have determined that the crust of the façade indicates the shaft was dug approximately fifty years ago. Malachi Baines is 45 years old. The tunnel was probably constructed before he was born."

"But," Prince interrupted, "It *was* dug specifically to sabotage the bridge site."

"No Harry. There is no conclusive data to support that theory. Quite the contrary. In the 1930's and 40's numerous short mining shafts were hand dug in that mountain to mine coal. Look closely at this next shot. The arrows on the screen indicate an exposed vein of coal in this shaft and clear evidence that coal has been extracted from the vein in the past." Striking his best oratorical pose, the animated lawyer continued. "The tunnel was constructed on a deeded private easement belonging to the Baines family since 1921. The roadway is private property. All previous bridges have been private property. The fact is the collapsed bridge was hastily constructed on private property under dubious legal authority! But, *regardless* of the original intent of the tunnel, under no circumstance can Malachi Baines be held responsible for an act committed prior to his birth!"

Harry Prince removed his over-sized glasses and vigorously wiped them with a white handkerchief. "Okay, even if Malachi Baines' grandfather dug the tunnel on his own land 50 years ago, even if it was originally a coal mine, even if the federal government over-stepped it's authority to build the new bridge…the fact remains that the

192

tunnel *was* flooded and this flooding *did* lead directly to the deaths of five officers. The U.S. Attorney contends that Baines alone had the motive, the opportunity and the know-how to flood the tunnel."

"The U.S. Attorney was under intense political pressure to produce a theory of motive and means. This *was* a very creative stretch on her part. Let's examine some more photos from the collapse site. The two large gullies in the middle of this eroded hillside channeled rain runoff from a 100 acre watershed down through three air shaft holes into the tunnel's main shaft. A flash flood torrent ultimately filled the cavern, putting water pressure on the tunnel's south wall, which started to slowly crumble. The added weight of the armored vehicles actually caused the compromised north bridge abutment to give way. Harry, there is zero proof of any human effort to channel the rain water runoff into the mine. During the federal grand jury proceedings, a 23-year-old graduate student from Alberta Canada testified that the erosion ravines were perfectly designed 'trenches' to direct water into the 'drainage shafts' and that both the trenches and the shafts appeared to be of very recent construction. His *professional* estimate was the trenches were built no more than 30 days prior to the incident." Riley called for a close-up photo of the gully to be shown. "Note the smooth curvatures of the crevasse and the arrows pointing to polished bedrock surfaces in the bottom of the ravines. Three highly regarded geologists have concluded the chasms were gradually sculpted by decades of natural water drainage. The so-called 'drainage shafts' were built 50 years ago. They were completely covered with vegetation. Harry, it was physically impossible for any human to direct the surface-water runoff into that old mining shaft." The tall attorney slammed his hand on the desk. "The U.S. Attorney's rationale for Malachi Baines 'opportunity and know-how' is just plain poppycock! Period!"

"Wow!" Harry Prince shook his head. "That is very convincing stuff counselor. Let's take a short break."

After the commercials, Prince said softly, "This whole fateful episode started with child molestation charges being leveled at Malachi Baines. Sources tell me a reliable witness recently observed Baines in a heated physical struggle with the child. Isn't there sufficient evidence to be concerned about the girl's well-being in that home?"

Summers responded harshly, "Absolutely not! There is not one shred of evidence to indicate the child is not perfectly safe with her parents. The initial allegation arose from a vague 30-second conversation reported by the local sheriff's wife. The high school principal who was privy to the report has confirmed that the child *did not* implicate her father. No one in law enforcement has discovered any information linking Malachi Baines to an inappropriate relationship with his daughter. As far as the alleged argument with his daughter – well let me just say, when my own daughter was 14, we had a dozen 'heated struggles' a week over everything from TV channels to her homework. There is certainly nothing inherently inappropriate…or even unusual…about that kind of exchange with a teenager!"

Prince nodded in agreement. "Oh yes, how well I remember having a teenager at home."

"Nevertheless," Riley responded somberly, "There remains the real concern that an adult outside her family *may* have harmed this child at some point. Unfortunately, the local sheriff – and more recently, federal officials – have so egregiously over reacted and mishandled the situation that the opportunity to properly investigate issues relating to the child's safety have thus far been lost."

"You have on several occasions tonight made reference to the local Summer County Sheriff, J.P. Jordan. You feel like he is largely responsible for this whole tragic mess don't you?

"Yes, I do! Without question. At the very least, Sheriff Jordan is guilty of poor judgment. He violated every tenet of law enforcement ethics by ordering a warrantless SWAT team raid under the pretense of a preliminary investigation. Sheriff Jordan's ill-advised actions lead directly to the deaths of four deputies and at least indirectly to the deaths of five federal agents."

Harry Prince folded his hands and raised his brushy eye brows. "Your family has a long history with Sheriff Jordan. Your late father was the Summer County District Attorney in the 1960's and 70's. I am told your dad investigated J.P. Jordan extensively but was never able to convince a local grand jury to indict the popular sheriff. Your father was later voted out of office, presumably due to his investigation of Jordan. What was that investigation about, and do you feel like you have an old score to settle with the Sheriff?"

"Harry I don't know many details about my father's work as the Summer D.A. I was very young during those years."

"But," Prince interrupted, "You *are* aware that your Dad had something on the Sheriff?"

"Let me just say my defense of Malachi Baines has absolutely nothing to do with J.P. Jordan's actions in the 1960's. It has everything to do with an innocent man being

195

railroaded to hanging-tree justice by over-zealous officials at both the local and federal levels."

Harry Prince nodded. "Fair enough counselor…you have a remarkable resume. You have successfully represented an eclectic mix of clients from the Arkansas Hacker to Hitler's henchmen. You have truly seen it all in your legal career. The recent events in Summer County are already the deadliest episode in the nation's law enforcement history. Now, dozens of Federal agents are poised to arrest Malachi Baines…apparently intent on charging his home with the full force of a small army. A local deputy is under indictment for shooting a fellow officer. Racial violence is spilling out into the streets of Westville. The Alabama National Guard is enforcing the equivalent of martial law. Protest marchers by the thousands. Politicians screaming for Malachi Baines' head on a platter. And still the unresolved question of who molested a young girl…Mr. Summer, what *is* going to be the final outcome in Summer County, Alabama?"

"Harry I hope and pray the final outcome is a victory for our American system of justice. If Malachi Baines loses his right to due process under the law…then we all lose a precious birthright."

TWENTY-THREE

Dye's Landing, Summer County   *9:00 am*   *July 1, 1998*

Ted made the sharp right turn onto the crunching surface of Dye's Landing road. The clean feel of an early summer morning swirled through his partially rolled down window. He took a deep breath of the woodsy air. Every tree and plant in his sight glistened in their varying hues of deep green. *Gosh this area is beautiful. What would it be like to actually "live" here? To have deep roots here? – For that matter, to have deeps roots anywhere.* His ringing cell phone quickly pulled him back into the only world he really knew.

Rocky's voice sounded tired. "Somehow J.P. has gotten a District Court judge to sign a search warrant for Dexter Grayson's home and gallery. The Sheriff's Department is going in with an FBI crime lab team tomorrow morning. But the county attorney has advised the sheriff that the warrant will never survive a higher court test. I tried to tell J.P. to hold up for more evidence and not risk screwing up the whole case. But I don't know. He seems more concerned about doing something the press will cover than building a solid criminal case. You know *I believe* Dexter molested Callie and a lot of other kids, but this search could get any evidence they collect tossed out later.

Associated Press Wire Service   *11:15 am*   *July 2, 1998*

Local sources have confirmed the Summer County Sheriff's office and the F.B.I. have executed a search warrant at a local residence in connection with the alleged molestation of a minor. The A.P. has learned the search has a direct connection to the seven-week long episode that has resulted in the deaths of four sheriffs' deputies and five federal agents.

Dye's Landing, Summer County   11:30 am   July 2, 1998

Brad Cowan took a seat on Rocky's faded sofa and gestured toward his A.B.I. partner. "Rocky, Ted, this is Bill Wadkins. I trust him with my life." The agent tossed a brown folder on the cypress knee coffee table. "It's all here. The slug we dug up at the attack site had blood and bone fragments from the black dog that was shot at point blank range…the dog that was latched onto Dave Ellis." Brad hesitated and looked at Rocky. "And that slug was *not* fired from Dave Ellis' weapon…it was matched to Buck Yancey's Glock!"

Rocky sprang out of his recliner and started pacing. "This black dog was definitely shot point blank in Dave Ellis' lap. Only Dave himself could have fired the bullet at that angle…but it was fired from Yancey's piece. Dave Ellis must have used Buck Yancey's weapon!" Rocky stopped pacing and stared at Ted. "That means the same gun that killed the black dog fired the slug that killed Willie Gaddis…the gun that Dave Ellis was firing!"

Ted stood up and retrieved Cowan's folder. "It also probably means Buck Yancey was firing Ellis' gun. That would explain why the white-headed dog Buck says he shot was killed with a slug from Ellis' gun. Buck says he only fired his Glock twice. Dave Ellis' Glock was missing two rounds. Buck's weapon was missing five rounds."

Brad nodded. "We checked and double checked. Amazingly, both those Glocks are completely free of prints. It's like somebody at the scene deliberately wiped them clean of even a single partial print."

"And," Wadkins added, "according to the sheriff's incident report, these two weapons were found lying two feet apart on the ground near where Yancey was giving first aid to Ellis."

Rocky slammed his left fist into his open right palm. "Yes! That's because when Ellis stopped firing and collapsed, his weapon would have dropped on the spot. Buck says, after he shot the last dog off his legs, he crawled over to Ellis and applied direct pressure to his wound. Buck never re-holstered his piece and would have had to lay down the gun to use both hands on Ellis…Most likely Buck laid it down right beside where Ellis' gun dropped. Without prints, it is impossible to tell which guy dropped which gun."

Ted fished a small tattered notebook out of a cargo pocket and started flipping pages. "When I interviewed Buck Yancey, he said he was wearing gloves during the whole incident…and that Ellis also had on gloves."

"That's right," Wadkins agreed, "When the other deputies arrived at the scene, both Yancey and Ellis were wearing blood-soaked shooting gloves. Our lab matched the blood on all four gloves to Dave Ellis."

Brad interjected, "The gloves would explain why neither Glock picked up prints during the attack, but why were they clear of any previous prints?"

Ted flipped another page. "According to Yancey, the day before the attack, Yancey, Gaddis, Ellis and Jock Norris all shot targets together at a local range. Are their weapons similar? Could they have gotten exchanged at the range?"

"They're not just similar," Wadkins answered, "they're *identical*. Yancey and Ellis' service weapons have consecutive serial numbers, were purchased in the same batch by the Sheriff's department, and issued to Yancey and Ellis on the same day, February 7, 1996."

"Let's go!" Rocky said. "I think Ted's got it pegged. We need to talk to ole Roosevelt out at the Coosa Gun Club."

Coosa Gun Club, Summer County   *1:00 pm*   *July 2, 1998*

The four large men descended on the snow-haired little black man in a rush of urgency. He looked around his creaky rocking chair startled by all the sudden attention.

Rocky patted his stooped shoulders. "Rosie how you doing?"

He looked up through blood shot eyes. "Weel Mista Rocky, ole Arthur-rite-us got me now in both knees and sugar done et up my blood, but I'm still here."

"Rosie, we need your help. Do you remember the day last month that Willie Gaddis, Buck Yancey, Dave Ellis and Jock Norris came out here together to shoot?"

"Oh yessuh! I's never gonna forgit dat day. It was da day afore all de sheriffs got kilt by dem dogs."

"Rosie, did all the deputies shoot targets with their own service weapons?"

"Yessuh. Shonuff did. Three of dem po-lice guns was jest alike."

200

"What made you notice the guns were the same?"

"I knows dey was jest alike 'cause I cleaned 'em all up and oiled 'em down *fine* when deys was done. You know Mista Rocky, jest like I's always wiped down yo gun with oil. Deys got all done shoot'n and went over to tha riva bank to have some beer. Fore dat dey laid dem fo guns right der on tha counter foe me to clean. I tole 'em to keeps em in order foe me. Mista Dave's was fust, den Willie's, den Mista Bucks and Mista Jock's. I got em one at a time, wiped em up and put em back in jest that same order."

Rocky knelt down to the old man's eye level. "Did you pay attention when they picked up their weapons and holstered them?"

"Yessuh. I remember dat cuz Mista Dave was bein so crazy. Mista Jock took his gun fust and put it 'way. I sho'd Willie his and he took it, but den Mista Dave sez he wants tha best one left and grabs for Mista Bucks'. Dey is both laughin an pushin an mixin dem guns all up. Dey finally somehow gets one each. I guess it don't matter 'cause deys both jest alike."

Rocky stood up and looked solemnly at Brad. "Rosie, were any of the guys wearing shooting gloves that day?"

"Yessuh. They shonuf was. Dem foe sheriffs always wears gloves out here."

"So they *all* still had gloves on when they loaded and re-holstered the guns after you cleaned them up?"

"Yessuh. Dey all had 'em on when dey lef dis shed."

The small man wrinkled his ebony brow and stared out across the river. "Lawdy, Lawdy, Mista Rocky. What's done happened here? Dis used to be such ah fine place foe both white folks and de colored folks to live. We don't needs loud mouth colored preachers from New York City spreading hate 'tween good nabors. I's don't believe Mr. Buck kilt Willie." He turned his gaze on Rocky. "I knows something dat not many black folks nor white folks even knows. Peoples trust you Mista Rocky. I wants you to spread dis word. Las year when Willie's boy Demarcus got sick, dey said he was gonna die if he dint get ah new kidney. All da Gaddis' got bad kidneys. Too bad to put in da boys body. No colored folk round here offered much help. Mista Buck's boy, Matt, jest on his own, sez Demarcus could have one of his. Dem two boys been bestest friends since fust grade. Mista Buck said Matt could do it, but it had to be a secret. Da Yancey boy was in Bumingham two weeks, an nobody cept the Gaddis' ever knowed why. Demarcus Gaddis is walkin' 'round cause he got Matt Yancey's kidney tied in him. Dat's da way it'spose to be. Tha good Lawd don't see white peoples and color peoples. He jest sees us all da same. Dis county knowed dat 'fore dem dogs got da sheriffs."

U.A.B. Medical Center   *Birmingham, Alabama*   *6:00 pm*   *July 2, 1998*

Brad Cowan, Bill Wadkins, Rocky and Ted squeezed into a visitation room in the hospital's psych ward. A young man with shoulder length hair trailed the four men into the windowless room. He appeared to be around 18, but had MD after his name on the white lab coat.

"Physically, Mr. Ellis has progressed well from his trauma. He is scheduled for a series of reconstructive surgeries starting next week. Emotionally however, he is struggling. He communicates for short periods of time, then lapses into periods where he does not speak or apparently hear for hours. Many of his symptoms fit the classic pattern for post-traumatic stress syndrome. We will just have to see if he will talk with you today."

In a few minutes, a nurse rolled Dave Ellis into the sterile, colorless room. He was a pale man with short silver hair and wire-rimmed glasses with more the appearance of a college professor than a cop. He seemed alert, but oblivious to the room full of visitors.

Rocky took his right hand and gave it a hard squeeze. "Dave, it's me, Rocky. It's great to see you. These other guys are ABI agents and a reporter. Will you talk to us for a few minutes?"

Ellis looked at Rocky's face for the first time. Teardrops began a slow slide down his cheeks. "Rock," he said softly, "Do you know what happened to me?"

Rocky swallowed hard and grasped his hand again. "It's okay, they're going to help you. You're going to be okay buddy. Can you tell us what you remember about the attack?"

Ellis sniffed and wiped his nose with a tissue he had been gripping tightly in his left hand. "The first big dog had Lem on the ground before I saw what was happening. I drew my weapon and tried to get a clean shot. There was so much movement and brush in between…twice I almost touched off. I came so close to taking that dog out. I stepped forward to see around a bush. Just as I raised my gun, I got hit below the waist. I didn't even…" He sniffed again and dabbed both eyes with the tissue, then continued in his low measured voice, "I didn't even realize it was a dog at first. It was like being hit by a truck…then the pain. It ran from my feet to my head…like hot pokers all through my body. I just instinctly put my barrel directly on the animal and shot it. Then, for just a brief second, I thought I was okay. I didn't think I was really hurt. Then I saw the blood and the pain shot through me again. It was so bad…I think I cried out. It got worse and worse."

Ted glanced around the room at the other men. You could feel the common empathy for the torturous experience Dave Ellis had endured.

"I staggered backward…and then I saw the white-faced dog pulling Willie's arm like it was a rag. A black dog with blood on its mouth was behind Willie – lunging at him, biting him over and over and over. I was shaking so hard, trying not to fall." Dave shut his eyes and gripped his wheelchair arms with both hands. His face contorted into a pained expression. "When I close my eyes, I'm always there again. Willie's on the ground, bleeding, crying for help. The dogs are all over him. I try to make my arms stop shaking. I try to shoot, but I can't make my finger pull the trigger. I'm pulling so hard…so hard, but it won't shoot. I can't see Willie anymore. I can't see the dogs. Everything is dark. The gun finally fires and fires and fires. Now it won't stop. I can't make it stop!" He sobbed, "God in heaven, have I shot Willie?" He shook violently, then slumped silently into a still, comatose state before the doctor rolled him out of the room.

Later, the four men sat quietly with their coffee around a small table in the hospital cafeteria. Ted lit a cigarette. "So, Dave Ellis accidently shot Willie Gaddis with Buck Yancey's weapon that was swapped at the range. It's clear why neither weapon had fingerprints."

"Yeah," Wadkins agreed as he flipped through a file, "and a shot fired from Ellis' position fits the bullet channel in Gaddis' body. It was always a stretch to argue that Yancey could have fired a shot from the right side of Gaddis."

Brad gestured at Ted with his Styrofoam coffee cup. "We're glad you've got all this down. You're the big insurance policy for me and Bill. What we've found today might never see the light of day at the ABI. The director's not going to like it. The AG's not going to like it. Best case, Bill and I will be pulled off this investigation and they will sit on our report until after the election. We may even get canned over this. With what we've got now, the AG will be forced to drop his indictment of Buck Yancey."

"Yeah," Rocky added, "and that asshole agitator Lucius Cockrell will have to pack it in!"

Ted blew a stream of smoke straight up toward the florescent tube lights. "I promise you Brad that Monday morning, 5 million copies of Newslink will detail the true story of Willie Gaddis' death."

Rocky ran a hand through his short hair and looked around the table. "What a damn irony. Dave fired the bullet that killed Willie Gaddis and set off this black backlash. The majority of *his* friends are black. Most of the whites in Summer County have snubbed Dave his whole adult life for having a black wife and family."

TWENTY-FOUR

Piney Bald, Summer County   *12:00 midnight*   *July 3, 1998*

The white moon beams filtered through the numerous cracks in the rough hewn log shack. The small stooped torso was covered head to toe with a burlap robe colored solid red with dried blood. Granny Tate held up a single corn shuck figurine in her bony right hand. The tiny mannequin had a wide black strip of tape at the waist and crude boots crafted from more black tape on its legs. Its head dripped with fresh warm dove's blood. She pointed her left index finger toward the moon and chanted. "Mother of the stars, mother of the skies, mash tha devil man's brains et hurt my Callie! Burn his rotten soul in tha fires of hell! Afore tha moon is full, tha deed be done! Tha deed be done!"

Tate's Gap, Summer County   *11:30 am*   *July 3, 1998*

The Cane Ridge Mountains morning haze gave way to a blue-bird mid-day sky. The hillside forests were awash in multiple shades of summer green. Just before noon, the pastoral setting near Tate's Gap was transformed into a scene from a war movie. Military helicopters lifted off in droves from the FBI staging area. The reverberating whir of the choppers could be heard for miles. They formed two lines in flight and roared up the mountain like a swarm of hornets toward Piney Bald. The Federal Government had lost its patience with the Malachi Baines stand-off. Over one hundred heavily armed special agents and U.S. Marshals were being air-lifted into Baines' front yard. The arrest warrant would be executed in just minutes at all costs.

From Malachi Baines' front porch, the ominous sound of the charging helicopters grew closer and closer like a fast approaching rain storm. Four gunships hovered in positions surrounding the cabin and a loud speaker ordered Baines to walk into the yard with his hands up. The man rocking on the front porch was clearly visible to the helicopter pilots, but he made no effort to comply with the repeated orders. Shortly, the other choppers began to land one by one on the flat plateau around the little cluster of buildings. Men in full combat gear leaped out and took defensive positions nearby. They stormed into Granny Tate's shack and the barns near the main house. As more commandos disembarked, they reinforced and tightened the circle around the Baines' home. The denim clad man on the front porch was in the cross-hairs of dozens of sharp-shooters on the ground and in the air. Tense agents had trigger fingers poised.

J. Riley Summer serenely puffed a large cigar and slowly swayed in the hand-made rocker. He smiled and shook his head. The bravado show of police might greatly amused him. When he raised his arm to thump off cigar ashes, the closest commandos took the slack out of their triggers. A trio of agents brandishing automatic weapons inched closer to the porch. When he ignored their order to stand up, they rushed him.

The agents roughly jerked up the attorney and slammed him against the wall, frisking him from head to toe. "Hey! Hey! I don't have a weapon, but I do have a court order your boss needs to see." He twisted free and shoved a folded piece of paper into a commando's face. The agent snatched the paper and demanded to see ID. "I'm Malachi Baines' lawyer," he said, "and I'm here as an officer of the court." He pulled out his driver's license and tossed it at the feet of the fatigue-clad marshal. Six other commandos rushed through the open cabin door and made a quick search. "Don't touch a damn thing in the house!" he shouted, "I'm holding a court injunction against any search or seizure."

Within seconds, an FBI commander was glaring at Summer. "If you're harboring a fugitive, it's…"

"Save your breath," Riley interrupted, "I know the law. Read the damn document. Judge Lambert says Malachi Baines has until noon today to present himself to the U.S. Marshal's office in Nashville." Summer glanced at his watch. "I believe if you'll make a call, you can verify that the entire Baines family is in the protective custody of the U.S. Marshal Service. Make sure your men don't remove any items from this property. Judge Lambert is also very clear on that point." The ruddy-faced lawyer returned to his rocker, retrieved his cigar from the floor and re-lit it. He blew a cloud of gray smoke toward the group of combat ready agents. "That's great mascara you guys have on. Does it itch?"

Sandy Creek Road, Summer County   *10:00 am*   *July 4, 1998*

Jarvis Whitfield's vintage Studebaker chugged along in a first gear snail's pace down the narrow sandy road. Even with the windows down the old car retained the stale smell of a shuttered attic. The grey-bearded professor gripped the steering wheel tightly with both wrinkled hands and stared intently ahead for the next pothole. When Ted

shifted to look at Jarvis, he felt a spring under the faded vinyl poke his bottom.

"I appreciate the invitation and the ride, but I've got a plane to catch and I've

thought all morning we might be wasting our time to witness a publicity stunt. Rightly or

wrongly, Buck Yancey is still facing a murder indictment. He certainly would not be the

first accused felon to suddenly find Jesus! And do you really believe Tonya is ready to

swap lap dances for prayer meetings?"

Jarvis kept his eyes focused on the winding bumpy lane. "I think this is a genuine

conversion. If it was about publicity, they would have gone to a large white church in

town and called CNN. Brother Terrell believes Buck has truly repented from his vulgar

racist ways. I've also heard reports that Tonya's testimony is very compelling."

They rounded a curve and saw a line of trucks and cars parked on the brushy

shoulder. Jarvis meticulously maneuvered into a parking spot and pulled on the

emergency brake with an annoying shriek.

Ted pushed open the stiff passenger side door and stepped out into a low tangle of

thorny vines. *Crap! I hope the dog and pony show is worth all this damn trouble!*

Jarvis paused in the road and wiped the dust off his wire-rimmed glasses with a

powder blue handkerchief. "Follow me to the bridge. You will likely be the only

reporter to witness this event. Please keep your camera out of sight!"

Ted followed Jarvis' plodding footsteps a short distance to where the dirt road

crossed a one-lane bridge. A few dozen people already lined the rusty railing on the

bridge's east side. When the two approached the overlook, several people scooted aside

to give them a choice view of the meandering stream, fifteen feet below. A short distance down the left bank, a sizeable crowd had gathered in an open clover field just feet from the steep bank of Sandy Creek. The group was a patchwork mixture of blacks and whites of all ages. Nearly all of the black people were dressed in Sunday church attire while many of the white men were tie-less in open shirts and jeans. Several dozen women of both races held open umbrellas to shield the morning sun.

Jarvis keenly studied the crowd for several minutes before whispering, "You and I are probably the only two people on this creek who have *not* spent our entire lives in Summer County." He pointed to a white teenager standing shoulder to shoulder with a black teen. "See those two young men in the blue and green shirts? That's Buck's son Matt and Willie Gaddis' son Demarcus."

Ted nodded. "That's a dramatic sight."

There was no apparent racial clustering anywhere on the thick carpet of crimson clover. It seemed to be about a fifty-fifty mixture and they were all chatting and laughing together. Two young girls, one black the other white, were handing out small brown books.

Ted looked away from the people and down the winding stream. *What an incredibly beautiful spot!* The stark white bark of majestic sycamores on both banks towered over the caramel-colored water. Below the massive sycamore limbs, thickets of cottonwoods were in full bloom, their clusters of snow white petals showcased against bright green summer foliage. The whole area radiated with the intoxicating scents of privet hedge and honeysuckle blossoms.

He heard musical notes from down below. A black man in a blue suit was seated at a piano atop a flatbed farm truck parked near the creek bank. Ted squinted his eyes.

210

That is the same guy from the Westville Church that played for the Willie Gaddis funeral!

A thin white woman in a pink dress and straw hat stood on a flat rock to lead the singing. People opened the little brown books. Singing voices filled the fresh morning air. *"Have Thine own way, Lord! Have Thine own way!"* Everyone grouped together to share the hymn books. An older white woman and young black man shared a single book and all sang at the top of their lungs. *"Search me and try me, Mas-ter, today!...Whit-er than snow, Lord wash me just now...As in Thy pres-ence humbly I bow."*

When the soulful singing stopped, a short chunky black man in a purple robe was helped down the slippery bank and into the water. Ted realized he was one of the A.M.E. preachers at the Gaddis funeral. He waded out a few feet and turned to face the assembly.

"Brothas 'n' Sistas in Christ we is here dis day on a joyful occasion! Rejoice with me!" A chorus of 'Amens!' and 'Hallelujahs!' rolled out from the group. "We is here dis day to cel-e-brate tha merciful salvation of our Savoir and Lord, Jesus Christ! We is here dis day to cel-e-brate tha redemption of our sista Tonya and our brotha Buck!"

More 'Amens!' rang out. "Come on down to da riva of mercy sista Tonya!" Tonya Yancey clad in a white robe walked out of the crowd. Two black men in suits and ties, seemingly oblivious to the mud and water soiling their fancy clothes, led her down the sharp drop off and all the way out to the preacher.

The minister put his left hand on Tonya's waist and turned her perpendicular to the group facing up stream toward the bridge. "Merciful Savior wash our sista Tonya in tha blood of tha lamb." He twisted and slid his left hand up to the back of her neck and placed his right hand in the middle of her chest. She pinched her nose and went limp as

211

the preacher pushed her whole upper torso under the muddy surface. He quickly raised

her back up and shouted, "Be cleansed of ya sins Sister Tonya! Hallelujah! Hallelujah!"

Cries of 'Hallelujah' and 'Praise the Lord!' came from the crowd which had edged up

closer to the creek. Tonya still facing the bridge arched her back and pushed her long,

wet hair back behind her head with both hands. The thin white robe clung skin tight to

her large round breasts. The leather skinned farmer standing to Ted's right took off his

sunshades and muttered, "Goodness gracious!"

The preacher kept his left arm around Tonya's waist and turned her back toward

the crowd. He pointed his short right arm toward the sky and cried out right in her ear,

"Praise the Lord! This sista is born again! This sista is born again!" This time four male

church assistants, clad in their Sunday best, splashed out to assist Tonya's exit out of the

creek and back up the bank.

The excited assembly was still applauding and shouting over Tonya's redemption

dip when Buck Yancey appeared at the edge of the high bank. Buck's white robe only

covered him to the top of his knees. His new pink scars were visible down to his toes.

The preacher in the stream shouted, "Come on down brotha Buck! Tha day of

redemption is at hand!" With the help of two wet and muddy ushers, Buck started

gingerly down the slick incline. He lost his footing and slid on his bottom feet first into

the dingy water dragging both assistants down with him. They all splattered and

struggled to their feet then slowly made their way out to the waiting minister. He stood

in waist-deep water that barely covered the tall deputy's knees.

The preacher placed his left hand on Buck's lower back. "Merciful Savior wash

our brotha Buck in tha blood of tha lamb!" He stretched his right hand up as high as possible to reach Buck's shoulder and coached him into a half turn toward the bridge. Buck then squatted and collapsed backward in a large submissive splash under the preacher's hands. The big man popped up and staggered to his feet coughing and spitting out water. Two hundred black and white voices shouted, "Hallelujah!" over and over in unison. The preacher grabbed Buck's hand and screamed, "Be cleansed of ya sins brotha Buck! This brotha is born again!"

The reporter in Ted could not resist any longer. He pulled his camera out and took three quick shots. Jarvis gave him an icy glare.

The soaked ushers pushed and pulled Buck back up the bank then returned to assist the preacher out of the creek. The pianist began to play and everyone gathered around the song book holders again. *"Mine eyes have seen the glo-ry of the com-ing of the Lord; He is trampling out the vintage where the grapes of wrath are stored."* Blacks were hugging whites and whites were hugging blacks. Some mixed groups were hugging and singing at the same time. Many were crying. Ted felt a chill running down his spine.

"Glo-ry, glo-ry, hal-le-lu-jah! Glo-ry, glo-ry, hal-le-lu-jah! Glo-ry, glo-ry, hal-le-lu-jah! Our God is marching on."

Ted spotted Buck Yancey with one large arm around his son and the other around Willie Gaddis' son.

Jarvis turned and looked at Ted. The stoic old professor had tears running off his face. "This is amazing, truly amazing."

The voices sang out over and over in the lush summer beauty of the tranquil creek bottom. *"He has sounded forth the trumpet that shall nev-er sound re-treat; He is sift-ing out the hearts of men before His judgment seat..."*

213

FINAL CHAPTER

Dye's Landing, Summer County   *12:00 noon*   *July 4, 1998*

Ted propped on an elbow on the concrete picnic table and enjoyed a long draw on his cigarette. *If Callie Baines names Dexter Grayson this is over! Forty-three straight days in this place called Summer County. What a run. What a story. If I can just do the finale justice, maybe this is finally it. The big one that didn't get away. It's not Watergate, but it could be bigger. It's gritty, it's human, and it's about real pain. But is it really over? Cher will have to listen for days to every little detail.*

At the sound of popping gravel, Ted turned to see the familiar state SUV pull up next to his packed rental car. Skeeter and Rocky got out and walked toward him. Ted pulled off his sunglasses and grinned. "One of you two looks absolutely gorgeous today."

Skeeter smiled and held back a swath of her glistening hair with her left hand. "I'm sorta gonna miss you 'round here. You lie to a woman better than any man I've ever seen."

Ted chuckled, "Well darling, I'm going to tell you one more and say I'll be back down here real soon to drink coffee with you." Ted stood up and crushed his cigarette butt under his foot. "Well guys, even though I get a lot of practice, I've never been very good at good-byes. So, I think I'll just head to the Birmingham airport and mail you a postcard later."

Rocky extended his hand and Ted shook it. The game warden stepped back then grabbed Ted in a crushing bear hug. "You're a damn good guy for a Chicago yankee."

"Well, you're a pretty good guy yourself for a backwoods deer cop." The couple followed Ted up to his car. He looked at Skeeter, then at Rocky. "If I hug this good-looking girl and force her to give me a real kiss will I get arrested?"

"Nah, I guess not. But you've got a 30-second limit and keep both hands where I can see them."

Ted and Skeeter embraced and *she gave him* a long kiss on the mouth. He climbed in the car and clicked into his seatbelt. Skeeter turned and slowly walked away. Rocky placed both hands on the top of the car and looked down at Ted. "So you're headed to see Cher Lavoe next week?"

"Yep, I miss her. We've got a lot to talk about." Ted cranked the engine and Rocky stepped back. Ted put the gear shift in drive then hesitated and looked up at Rocky. "Okay, the answer is 'yes'. I still love her. Yes. I will always love her." In just a few seconds all he could see in the rear view mirror was a cloud of reddish dust.

Birmingham, Alabama   *2:15 pm*   *July 4, 1998*

Ted phoned his Newslink editor as he approached the airport. Susan reacted like she was waiting for the call. "Ted! Glad you called. You have received something here that could be quite interesting. A courier just delivered a package for you…It's from J. Riley Summer. We haven't opened it yet."

"Hmmm, that is interesting Susan. I've got an hour before my flight. Please get someone to open the package and let me know what it is as soon as you can."

"You bet Ted. I'll call you back."

Summer, Alabama   *2:30 pm*   *July 4, 1998*

Rocky walked into the sheriff's office and looked around. Everything seemed eerily quiet for a holiday with a double shift on duty. Day sergeant Frank Lipscomb motioned for Rocky to enter his office. "Rock, I just heard that Callie Baines gave a statement in Nashville and identified her assailant. I guess they haven't passed that down to us yet. J.P.'s been on the phone all day with the U.S. Marshal's office."

"Where is J.P. now?"

"I don't know. He left here about 15 minutes ago."

Rocky walked back into the squad room and dialed a number on his cell phone. "Hey Marlene, do you remember the story you told me about seeing Callie and Malachi out at the old barn? Okay, on that day or any other day on your bus route, did you ever see anyone else out there? I mean phone company trucks, delivery men, road workers, anybody?"

"Well now Rocky, let me think about that. There's hardly ever anybody out there 'cept at the store…but you know the day I saw them fussing, there was a law car passed back by the store."

"A Summer County Sheriff's Department car?"

"Well yeah, I reckon it was, I mean it was brown like all y'alls cars."

"Was it headed south, back toward town?"

"Yeah, that's right."

"About what time did you see it pass Marlene?"

"Oh, I reckon 'bout four maybe four-fifteen."

"So was that about 30 minutes after you dropped off Callie?"

"Well yeah, I guess. It was just a little while before I got back in the bus and saw her with her Daddy."

"Could you see what deputy was driving the car?"

"Well no Rocky. I just saw it going down the road from inside the store."

"Listen, thanks a lot Marlene. If you can remember anything else, please give me a call."

Rocky's mind was racing as he approached Rita Jo at her dispatch desk. "Rita Jo, you know the GPS system we put in five cars last year?"

"Yes Rocky. When we first got it, I logged onto that page every day for 3 months and signed off on the daily shift maps…but J.P. said it was a waste of time, so I quit doing it."

"Do you know how to get into the history file on those maps?"

"Sure. J.P. thought I had disabled the system but it still records 24-7. Give me a few minutes." She turned to one of two computer monitors at her station and quickly pulled up the files. "What date are you looking for?"

"Let's look at the first four days of May this year."

"Okay."

Rocky pointed to the screen. "So this is the car ID number?"

"Yes."

"Okay. Show me the May 1st mapped route for each car in the system."

Rita Jo pulled the stored map routes up one by one.

"Okay, let's do May 2nd. Now the 3rd…those little blue numbers are the time the car was at each location on the map?"

Rita Jo turned and stared wide-eyed at Rocky. "This is making me nervous! What's the matter? What are you looking for?"

"I can't say just yet…let's finish the 3rd and the 4th.

She clicked up another map. Rocky felt a cold chill run through his body. His voice quavered. "Rita Jo, pull up the real-time locations right now. All cars."

She pleaded, "Rocky what's wrong? I know something's bad wrong!"

He swallowed hard. "For right now you have to trust me Rita Jo. I've gotta go. I'm code 3 to Tate's Gap. I won't need back-up."

Birmingham Municipal Airport   *2:45 pm*   *July 4, 1998*

Ted answered his cell phone and Susan started talking with excitement in her voice. "Ted, this is dynamite! Summer sent you an extensive file and journal his father, the D.A., compiled on J.P. Jordan in 1966 and '67."

"Holy shit! What's it all about?"

"John Summer was convinced that Jordan molested his niece, Elizabeth Rankin, from 1965 through 1967. Starting when the girl was 12."

"Jesus Christ! That ties this all together! Did the D.A. have a solid case?"

"It looks like he had one eye-witness and several reliable sources. He took it to a grand jury twice, but couldn't get an indictment. He was never able to get a statement from the girl. According to his journal, Elizabeth Rankin was scheduled to give a statement to police in Birmingham on July 5th 1967. John Summer thought she died in a Birmingham hospital from an apparent suicide on July 4th 1967. He wrote that his strongest case died with Elizabeth Rankin."

"That explains why Jordan went to such great lengths to hide the secret that his niece has been alive all these years."

"Yes it does, and John Summer had a lot of circumstantial evidence linking Jordan to rapes of at least two other young girls. Summer left the D.A.'s office a very bitter man. He was convinced that J.P. Jordan could never be indicted in Summer County."

"Susan, I've got to call Rocky Barnett. I'll see you tonight."

Tate's Gap, Alabama   *3:05 pm*   *July 4, 1998*

Rocky sped through the twisting turns up the mountain as his piercing siren echoed down into the deep green valleys. *This could not be real. It had to be a dream...a nightmare. The last six weeks were a surreal nightmare. A fast paced horror flick you could not escape. But this was the cruelest dream of all. It simply could not be*

219

true. The man he had idolized his entire life could not abuse a young girl. The man he knew like his own skin was not a cold-blooded child molester willing to let innocent men die to cover up his crime.

He grabbed his cell phone off the dash when it rang. "Ted, be quick, I can't talk."

"Yeah, I can hear you're code 3, but you have to know this! John Summer had positive proof that J.P. Jordan sexually abused his niece, Elizabeth Rankin, in 1966 and '67. The sheriff spent all that money and carried out this elaborate scheme for decades to conceal the fact she was still alive! Rocky, are you hearing me? There were other young girls as well. It was a pattern. You've got to look at J.P. Jordan for the Callie Baines rape!"

"I already know that Ted," Rocky said softly, "I'm afraid the worst for J.P., but you've got to hang up and just let me deal with this the best way I can."

When Rocky spotted the sheriff's car parked beside the old barn, he knew immediately his horrific nightmare was now his harsh reality. He leaped from his car and rushed inside the musty smelling structure. "J.P.! J.P.! Where are you?"

"Don't come any closer son," the familiar gravelly voice said calmly. "You need to leave me alone."

Rocky turned to his right and saw the big man standing on an elevated hay storage platform. He held his service revolver pressed tight against his temple. "J.P. please put down your gun. I'm here to help you," he pleaded, "We can work this out together."

"No son," J.P. said serenely, "I'm beyond help. I'm years and years beyond help."

"We can ride back to town together and talk this out, just like we've always talked things out."

"Not this time son. It's over for me. We both know I can't go back to town and face what's coming my way."

"J.P., did you have sex with Callie in this barn? Say it's not true! I'll get you a lawyer and fight for you with everything I've got!"

The old sheriff began to sob. "I wish I could tell you it's not true…but it is. I've been with her many times, and she's not the only one."

"But why J.P.? Why? I don't understand!"

"I'm so sorry. So sorry. You'll never know what it's like to be a grown man and feel like a bumbling boy all the time. But you listen to me. I don't deserve to live – I've caused good men to suffer and die. I've hurt kids. I'm nothing…nothing at all. You're my son. You're something special. I've failed my own dad, but you'll never fail me. You're the kind of man I wish I could have been. My dad would've been proud to call you his son."

Rocky was blinded by his own tears. He staggered toward the platform. "J.P. come over here and hug me. We can still get through this together."

"Son, please understand. Let me at least go out on my own terms. If you love me like a dad…give me this last dignity."

Rocky paused at the edge of the hayrack and looked up into J.P.'s face. Tears streamed down the young man's cheeks. "I do love you like a dad. You've always made me proud to say that." He turned and walked haltingly to the barn door, without looking back. The golden summer sunbeams highlighted the opening like spotlights on a center stage. He hesitated at the door and closed his eyes.

The gunshot reverberated up through the maze of webs into the mystical space known only to spiders and barn owls.

EPILOGUE

On July 7th 1998, the U.S. Attorney dropped the federal murder charges against Malachi Baines. He and his family happily returned to their Piney Bald home. Over 100 Summer townspeople volunteered their labor for three weeks to rebuild his private bridge. Malachi was rarely ever spotted again off his mountain.

On July 8th 1998, the state's murder indictment of Buck Yancey was withdrawn. Later the same day, Lucius Cockrell quietly dismissed his civil suit against Yancey and the Summer County Sheriff's Department.

On July 31st 1998, the state Attorney General and the A.B.I. officially closed their investigation into the dog mauling deaths.

In August of 1998, the U.S. Fish and Wildlife Service trapped and euthanized 11 feral dogs in Junee Bottoms.

Marabell Jordan moved to Beaufort, South Carolina on Labor Day of 1998.

Juanita Gaddis moved to Birmingham in October of 1998.

Dave Ellis eventually recovered from his injuries and moved with his family to South Florida in May of 1999.

In December 1998, J. Riley Summer was named Time Magazine's Man of the Year for his defense of Malachi Baines.

On June 1st 1999, following an Interpol sting operation, Dexter Lee Grayson and Dr. Colvin Dupree were arrested in Singapore on charges of sex-slave trafficking.

In July of 1999, Deputy Earlon "Buck" Yancey was ordained as a Baptist minister. On Easter Sunday 2000, Brother Buck was the guest preacher at the Westville AME church. Later that year he was named the Summer County Sheriff Department's first chaplain.

On November 3rd 1998, Hubbert Lester "Rocky" Barnett was elected sheriff of Summer County winning 88% of the ballots as a write-in candidate. Spud Jordan was retained as the department's chief deputy. The new sheriff immediately filled two openings in the department with African-American deputies.

In March of 1999 Rocky Barnett and Skeeter Yates were married in the Summer First Baptist Church. Ted Logan was the groom's best man.
Rocky and Skeeter bought a brick home in Summer and she gave birth to their first child, a son, John Powell Barnett in December 1999.

In October of 1998, Ted Logan won a Pulitzer Prize for his Newslink coverage of the events in Summer County.

In January of 1999, Ted Logan published his first book, <u>Dogs of Summer</u>, chronicling the Summer County saga. The book spent 42 weeks in 1999 at number one on the New York Times bestseller list.

In June of 2000, Universal Studio released the movie version of Logan's bestseller "Dogs of Summer." The box office smash starred Sam Elliott as Ted Logan, Dennis Quaid as Rocky Barnett, Demi Moore as Skeeter Yates, Larry Hagman as J.P. Jordan, James Caan as J. Riley Summer, and Robert Duvall as Malachi Baines.

On July 4th 2000, Ted Logan and Cher Lavoe were remarried in New York's Central Park

To read more background on the book and author as well as stay informed on future books, visit https://www.facebook.com/WBruceCanoles